*"A wonderful new novel . . .
bringing forth a magical sense
of San Francisco."*
—GAY COMMUNITY NEWS

"A spiritual-quest tale for gay men."
—THE ADVOCATE

LONGING

LONGING

Paul Reed

CELESTIAL ARTS
Berkeley, California

CELESTIAL ARTS
P.O. Box 7327
Berkeley, California 94707

Cover photo by Pete Macchia
Cover design by Ken Scott
Author photo by Savage Photography
Text design by Nancy Austin
Composition by Wilsted & Taylor, Oakland
Set in Baskerville

Library of Congress Cataloging-in-Publication Data

    Reed, Paul, 1956—
      Longing.
        p.   cm.
      ISBN: 0-89087-597-9 (pbk.)
      I. Title.
      PS3568.E369L66   1988
      813'.54—dc19   88-14994
                               CIP

First paperback edition, 1990

5   4   3   2   1
94 93 92 91 90

Manufactured in the United States of America

for Fred

LONGING

1

On Sunday evenings in San Francisco, one realizes that opportunities have come and gone. I sit at the window, just as I have always done, and when my arm against the sill goes numb, I know the weekend is truly over. It is a time when I wonder: Have I chosen the best path? Will I live long?

Long ago, when I had just moved to the city, the questions I asked by the window were different: Should I have spoken to that man last night at the Arena? Should I have stayed another half hour at Trocadero? The answers rarely mattered then—and matter less now—for after the sun reddens my face and the wind sweeps up from the ocean and down from Twin Peaks, I go home alone to watch the fog roll down the hills—so eerily timed, always, on Sunday evenings, as though to silence the revelry, carnival is done.

Sunday evenings always ordained our lives with a feeling of despair then, as though something precious had been irretrievably lost. Sometimes, in a fit of tenacity, we refused the counsel of languor and stubbornly pursued Sunday nights in that frantic, last-minute search for pleasure that earned its pursuers the tag "desperado." But inertia reigned for the most part—there was always time—so we abandoned Sunday afternoons in moods of complete dispassion.

Those afternoons were always spent in luxurious indecision anyway, as we declined invitations and watched the light fade, as we deferred decisions, passed over the matinee, and opted not to attend tea dance after all, we were too tired. So we sat idly on the bookstore steps or at Hibernia Beach, or at the bars along that two-block stretch of Castro Street, doing nothing, achieving nothing, feeling exactly like travelers adrift in the midst of a vacation that has gone on too long: the sights no longer engage us as they did.

At one time they had. When I had arrived after an adolescence spent in dusty hamlets, I was enthralled simply to be living amidst such overwhelming pleasure. To my newcomer's eyes the city was ripe with hedonism and rich with possibility. Men of my kind were everywhere, and the sharp, citified brusqueness filled me with excitement. Everything seemed foreign and mysterious. I remember how profound and wistful I felt my first night in San Francisco, when, in a handsome man's bed in the middle of the night, I looked out the window to discover that the regular strobes of light across the wall were cast by the searchlight on Alcatraz. And later I woke again to the melancholy call of the foghorn, deep and dolorous. I savored those first days in the city the way a child saves money—sparingly, greedily, awestruck. Everything was melodramatic to me: the crystalline shine of the ocean sky; the treeless stretches of endless pavement in certain parts of town; the vigor of climbing up and down hills; the prying eyes of handsome men assessing the new kid in town, fresh meat. I had arrived bitter with rejection and frustration—early life and schooling had proved lonely and plain, had shown me that I didn't fit in with the world of conformity and rural life, and I knew that in the city, at long last, I would find freedom, escape, perhaps release, certainly pleasure, and possibly love.

Every young man I met in the city had the same story to tell. We were a city of exiles, herded by that cold, mean wind into two or three neighborhoods from which we rarely departed. And each of those exiles had a tale to tell—stories of the unfulfilled promise of love so sad that I felt, at times, heartbroken with empathy.

My tale is one such story, colored by what I learned in those early years. Rather quickly I learned that yearning was everywhere present in the city, and love was its object. Longing permeated every mood and every action, a deep, aching desperation for something that seemed, perfectly, elsewhere. Once, while sunbathing atop a friend's building on a hot Saturday afternoon, I opened my eyes dreamily, propped myself up on my elbows for a moment, and delivered myself of the conclusion that denial gives rise to longing. My friend grunted and rubbed more coconut oil into his bronzed, bronzing thighs. "Look," I said, inclining my head toward the crowd below, thronging at the intersection of Market and Castro, "look how they shift and linger, waiting, hoping really, for someone, anyone—it's the thing that they were denied for such a protracted period of time that it's now

become a passion, an obsession, a goal in itself . . ." My
friend regarded the intersection for a moment, then
looked at me and said, "For Chrissakes! They're waiting
for the bus!" Then he reclined again and rolled onto his
left side, his back to me, his face towards the bay, Oakland, and Mount Diablo in the haze. "Look at that
freighter!" he exclaimed after a bit, and I did. A great
amber and grey freighter was making way, about to pass
beneath the Bay Bridge. It seemed to me the most desolate sight, so forlorn was I at the cheerless vision of an
ugly commercial vessel putting out to sea, as isolated and
lonely as the men in the intersection below. I had an image of the ship as it might be later that night in the open
sea, the merchant sailors below deck chummily drinking
beer, one of them strumming a guitar perhaps, lonely for
the girl he had left in Alameda. I watched it slip beneath
the bridge, the stern finally vanishing and relinquishing
the bay to the tiny white triangles of the sailboats that
drifted busily about the surface of the water. My friend
began to snore—he had fallen asleep in the sun. I lay
back and abandoned myself to melancholy, knowing that
yearning was life's purpose.

So I began my search for that which had been impossible elsewhere—the fulfillment of yearning, the
driving obsession for love. Later of course I learned that
obsession must be let go and yearnings must be abandoned. If held onto, they decay before your eyes like
those perfectly preserved mummies, which upon expo-
sure to the air crumble as the archaeologists look on,
frantic with helplessness. But the first time I had loved—
in college, just before moving to the city—I did not learn
to release yearning. Instead I savored it, embroidered

upon its manifestations—tears, prayers, hope, lingering—and brought it with me to the city.

But that was first love, frustrated and incomplete, a mere experimentation. When I loved again, it was fraught with desperation and more yearning. It was during that year the Castro gave its last gasp before succumbing to Change, the result of the terror of death. That year we still danced, so very much, until sweat poured from our shirtless bodies in those vast dance pavilions, late into the night, Saturday blending indistinctly with Sunday. That year we still fucked, too; the baths and sex clubs, so dark and warmly seductive, awaited, always, our arrival, en masse, those Friday and Saturday nights. How many years—accumulated from the shorter spans of hours and half-days—did we pass moving and shifting along those halls so packed with male flesh that one had, at times, to run breathless into the showers simply to escape the claustrophobic press of so many hungry men? That year one could still stand on the street and watch: tap dancers in full costume rounding the corner and dancing up the street; nearly nude men completing everything but orgasm in full view, in the light of day; three men dressed as the Andrews Sisters gliding up and down Castro Street in a 1972 Cadillac convertible, waving to passersby as though they were on parade. That year, too, a young Jewish man dressed himself as a female country singer and touted his act as "Patsy Klein," and, in an unrelated eventuality, several thousand men became fatally infected.

Then, amidst the consternation of panic and confusion, amidst the lessons of love, hope, and obsession, a young man fell in love with me, or so it seemed, and I with him. Is it ludicrous to liken a young man to an angel? He appeared suddenly and interrupted the chaos that life was becoming in the shadow of sexual drivenness and morbidity, obsession and fever. Love entered the scene then—long summer nights of quiet talk, murmuring sleep, missed phone calls.

It is a love story imbued now with the richness of recollection, a hazy edition of kisses, whispers, and memories so vivid and so enriched with romanticism that I can hardly endure a simple Sunday afternoon stroll down Castro Street without suffering a bittersweet poignancy. But memory is not reality, and the two must never be confused.

2

A romance is a love story, and stories have beginnings. For me, the beginnings were simple. There was little to know as a young man in a college town, even less to discover. The rhythms and habits of life are fixed in a place like that. There is no possibility of novelty, much less of violence, passion, sexuality. I had read my Faulkner, my Tennessee Williams, of course. But this was not the South. This was California—the interior. We had no heavy damp air, no swinging moss, no vibrating undercurrent of danger.

The college was located in the precise center of town. I had a room in a rambling house adjacent to campus, a house that I shared with nine other students. The campus stretched out behind the house like a wonderful large backyard, verdant in spring and summer, intricate with walkways, paths, and tangled trees in winter.

Summers made the gravest impression there, summers so long and so scorching that nothing moved except the dust and the fast, air-conditioned cars carrying people to cooler places. We sat for hours some afternoons, unable to move within that heat so thick it could be felt the way water drags as one steps into the sea against the tide. We would sit drinking iced tea or hot coffee (the story went that drinking hot beverages in warm climates raised the body temperature, thus making the air feel cooler to the skin), and we would pass the baking afternoons playing cards or backgammon, all in anticipation of dusk and the cool relief of darkness.

But all seasons make a difference in such a place, being primarily an agricultural region, and being full of trees and wind (the great outdoors began at one's front porch). The seasons were objects of scrutiny. Autumn was the finest season, when the town was bathed in orange haze and people complained bitterly of the suffocating smoke blown into town from the burning rice fields. As winter arrived, coats were pulled tighter, and lungs inhaled sharply at the scent of woodsmoke in the evening air.

Against this natural backdrop stood the college itself, the northernmost outpost of a huge educational bureaucracy that was nothing more than a factory for mass education. The practical thing, of course, would have been studies in business or computers, but I selected classical history and cultural anthropology—because these would offer a life of pure entertainment. The coursework was so light, and so vaguely, exotically interesting, that there was little to do but absorb what was presented.

Readings in classical literature intrigued me somewhat, but I was most distracted by ethnographic films that depicted primitive life in places like New Guinea, the Amazon Jungle, the Ivory Coast, India, East Africa—wonderful places where, I imagined, my greatest concern would be adjusting the shades of my hut against the afternoon sun.

Parties, too, filled vast spans of time. It seemed always as if the entire student body were at one party or another. A walk towards the clump of highrise dormitories produced, always, several invitations to beer busts and keggers, and being bored or curious, we often accepted, arriving totally unknown among a group of young men and women who, by eight or nine in the evening, were often quite drunk, some already vomiting.

Revelry permeated that college and that town, but sometimes things went too far, and we would read in the afternoon paper of a coed who had been raped by six or seven young men. Or worse, once a young woman was raped and strangled beneath the canopy of a spreading oak on a cool spring night. Or tragic, our friend—never recovered from his trauma in Viet Nam, yet making the most of his educational benefits anyway—took a revolver to his head in the parlor downstairs and blew his face off. But such tragedy was rare, indeed, for the prevailing inclination of the campus was to party.

So passed my freshman year.

During my sophomore year I arranged to attend classes on Tuesdays and Thursdays only, so I was often adrift in that cozy town, free to explore the university campus, its museums and galleries, and to rummage about the central commercial district, cramped with tiny shops and bars. I began, during that second year, to explore the vast entangled forest of a park that stretched from campus up into the rolling hills to the east, where a wild creek tumbled across huge, misshapen volcanic boulders and cut its way into the tamer, verdant woods that intersected town. By the time the creek reached campus, it was a slow, cold rivulet, meandering through a shallow creekbed and grasses, shadowed under ancient oaks and cottonwoods, their leaves rustling in occasional breezes.

Those trees were thick and tall, and I would find a clump of oaks whose roots were so gnarled and exposed by erosion that they formed makeshift chairs. I would sit, alone or with friends, legs dangling above the water. There we read serious books—Proust, Woolf, and Sartre—and we talked and stared across the lawns or wild grasses and grew sullen with reflection. Alone, I would stare, hypnotized, at the passing water, thinking that the town was lacking, that perhaps the state college was not for me. But I stayed on, out of curiosity, disinclined to move elsewhere, somehow rooted to the hope of possibility. There might be someone.

I discovered a section of the park called the grove, a snarled stand of cedars, redwoods, pines, oaks, cypresses, and sycamores. Close to the ground dense shrubs and vines interlaced to form thickets of greenery so heavy that sound and sight were obscured. The park department had installed a nature trail, which provided a twisting maze through the dense shrubs, with dozens of tiny private resting areas carved out of the otherwise impenetrable jungle adjacent to the trail.

A stroll through the grove in the afternoon or at night offered many possibilities, and this was the life I began to lead. There was nothing else. My knees were often dusty then, when I would stand after an evening in the grove and brush pine needles and broken leaves from my pants. Phone numbers were rarely exchanged. Secrecy prevailed. Entire sex acts were completed outdoors, the open air providing caresses in the absence of a lover. Some nights, long past midnight, I would sneak quietly back home and into the shower. Dust and twigs and leaves had to be washed from my clothes, my hair, my body. Then I would slip into bed and awaken to a house full of chattering young students, my housemates, each of them oblivious to my nocturnal life.

My third year in college was pivotal, for I suddenly began to indulge myself with abandon: sleeping until noon at the start of the term; perusing the library for hours, reading the foreign newspapers and the papers from New York, Boston, and Los Angeles; discussing John Updike and Lillian Hellman late into the night; smoking cigarettes and drinking; slipping into the grove after midnight, kneeling till three in the morning.

Some days I did nothing but sleep until five in the afternoon, perhaps reading in bed for a few minutes before dozing again. Then, after supper, I would walk the town, alone or with a housemate. We walked from one end of that flat town to another, observing the retired farmers watering their lawns and peach trees in early evening; seeing elderly folks rocking back and forth on their front porches, the old white paint of their houses chipped and cracked, as wrinkled as their skin; feeling the afternoon warmth give way to the evening breeze, whispering in the dry leaves of the elms and maples that lined so many of the town's streets; wandering into newer sections of town, filled with stucco tract houses and three-story apartment buildings. Sometimes, entire sections of almond orchards vanished, as if overnight, and next appeared busy clumps of modern apartments, each with a two-car garage. At one moment we would be walking through shadowed, muddy orchards, which, in the next, opened to a parking lot and sixty redwood decks overlooking us. Closer to downtown, as we returned to the university, we would pass groups of heavyset matrons en route to a meeting of the Rebekahs or Soroptimists, their long, glittering evening gowns so out of place on those small, hot sidewalks lined with pickup trucks, vans, and jeeps. Closer to campus the beer halls could be heard, loud rock or disco vibrating the walls, and as we neared our house, next to campus, the rows of fraternity and sorority houses issued raucous laughter, shrieks, and squeals of inebriate hilarity.

As another autumn took hold that third year, easing us into a new semester and edging the dry heat of summer behind us, I found myself indulging my new abandon at more and more parties. One party that fall was significant, for it contained the moment that precipitated the series of events that led, in time, to my exile from that dusty place.

Lately there had been what we called a southern sky. A southern sky is not blue. It is a glowing, hazy white— humid, warm, subtropical. I stood on a veranda with an enormous party in a high uproar behind me and studied an October sunset, or really, the last discernible moments of one, the pale pink haze yielding to an indigo descending like a heavy theater curtain about to smother the horizon. Behind me, inside, people were laughing and carrying on, satisfying intemperate urges in bursts of singing and dancing. At one point I took a proferred joint, inhaled deeply, and realized that the thing was dusted. Oh, well, I told myself, there go the next three days.

I had come with my friend and housemate Ann, who was, at that moment, sprawled across the top of a grand piano, leading a small collection of coeds in a round of show tunes. Already dizzy from the dust, I peered into the room to catch her eye and wave a warning, but then I caught sight of a young man inside the house, beyond a pair of french doors, beyond the group of singers. The sight of him stunned me. I started to smile, but—oh, the drug—silence . . . a brief meeting of the eyes . . . a turning towards the river.

Concentration eluded me, so I stared down from the veranda at the river, which, at that point, below the house, below the veranda, curved smoothly, directing the silted water around a clump of knotty, rooted sycamores. I stared at the water as long as I could, its gentle curve and smooth movement easing the tingling of my nerves, until I began to feel my head swim and was tempted to jump. I held tight to the railing and turned back to the party. The drug was making a haze of the evening, but I didn't mind.

That young man appeared again, closer, near the doors. I smiled and reached out, found that he was actually beside me. He introduced himself as Stephen. I smiled again, my eyes glazed. I said nothing.

The evening passed in a blur, until finally, just before midnight, Ann and I made excuses and walked home through the countryside. We looked up at the stars and the moon. We felt the edge of the drug wear off, our senses returning.

"That stuff makes me a lunatic," Ann said. I agreed by nodding my head and saying, "It's not nice not to warn you when it's dusted. It makes me crazy, too."

For a long time we were silent, the only sound our uneven footsteps resounding in varying tones against changing surfaces—gravel, dust, concrete, grass. I kicked a pebble along the road for a distance.

"There's too much to life," Ann volunteered in that manner we all adopted in college—contemplating the mysteries of existence in chitchat. She stopped beside an almond tree and looked up. She jumped and swatted at the branches. It rained wooden pellets.

We started walking again, and she went on: "You know, I dream about Europe and Africa and Australia and about running away to Paris all in a rush . . . I'd drop everything, sell my stuff—you know, the record player, the TV, that sort of thing—and just get on the next plane and *voilà!* There I'd be."

I laughed. Ann said things like *voilà* and got away with it. It was the huskiness of her voice, the solidity of her character. She always meant what she said. "Then why don't you?" I asked.

She said nothing. Then: "What was that?"

"Why don't you go to Paris?"

"Oh, *that* . . . well, because, you know, it's a day-dream, a cliché, that's all. It's a fantasy."

"Oh," I said. "I never dream like that."

"Like what?" asked Ann.

"Something so exotic, so far away. I do think about getting things I don't have, and going somewhere where things are different somehow, but not travel. . . ."

Ann shook her head.

I tried to clarify. "I mean that what I'm after has more to do with freedom than with locale." I meant sex with men.

She shrugged her shoulders. We were drawing close to town anyway, and I stopped thinking and listened to the night sounds around us—the ceaseless clatter of crickets, the scratch of wind in the dry almond groves. Moonlight cast odd shadows—mulatto ghosts in the woods—as we stepped through the trees, shortcutting to the other road into town, and we stepped lightly across sticky mud, the day's irrigation lingering in the soil and emitting must, woody and damp. I had no idea what time it was, but the air was warm and heavy, the occasional breeze dry and hot, the moonlight strangely vexing, not coolly luminous as I so loved it on sweet autumn nights.

We neared town, the scattered farmhouses giving way to apartment complexes and tiny, precise neighborhoods that yielded to busy streets and tidy lawns and cramped corner gas-marts illuminated in glaring fluorescent. Our mood was recast, the spell of moon-bathed nature broken, and we finally reached our street, noisy with collegiate revelry: cars, laughter, and music aimed at the street from second-story windows.

I couldn't sleep when we got home, so I walked another mile to the grove. I walked slowly against the warm breeze blowing down from the mountains and wondered when it would turn cold. When I reached the park I could see movement in the bushes, black forms. I crossed a roadway and entered the grove. I passed beneath a thick clump of magnolia trees, pushed my hands into my pockets and strolled into the woods. It seemed unusually still. I stopped and listened. Thick cypresses—dark sentinels against the night sky, no stars, the moon gone down—creaked in the wind, their branches groaning mournfully. Somewhere in the distance, far outside the park, tires squealed an angry rebellion against curfew.

Pine needles rustled to my left: footsteps. He came to me from a side trail and said hello. I turned my head and examined my visitor: a black moustache, a nervous tongue over lips, thick hands presenting himself. "Hello," I finally answered, my fingers pulling free of my pockets and taking hold. The display became practiced and theatrical then, our bodies rubbing in ceremony. His stubby fingers pressed me, encircled me—rough. I thought of a low ceiling of warm clouds. The sky was black. "Jesus Christ Almighty" I called out, dust on his knees. And then we were silent again, fever abating, the cypresses waving and creaking above.

"Keith," he said.

"Hello," I said again.

We pulled our pants up and sat on a log. I smiled at him and said, "I've never seen you here . . ."

He shook his head. "No, I've been afraid."

I nodded and tapped my foot against pine needles. High overhead an invisible airplane droned, then passed. A whisper walked behind us.

"Come to my place?" he asked.

I nodded and stood up.

We walked through the woods to a dirt parking lot. Teenagers leaned against their shiny cars and smoked. A car stereo blasted Emerson, Lake & Palmer. He shook his head at me and shrugged his shoulders. We climbed into a blue Mustang, a '68 or '69, I guessed, its immaculate navy interior and luminous wax job telling me everything I needed to know at that moment—what I would later come to call "butch." We pulled away from the park and turned onto that broad avenue I always took to walk home, and as we left a cloud of dust, one of the teenagers yelled something, we couldn't hear what, and suddenly I envisioned our precise situation there: The grove was but a fragile teacup in an arsenal of armor and missiles, as displaced and fragile as ceramic would be in a warehouse of iron, steel, and gunpowder. That men met, kissed, and separated within the few square yards of the grove's boundaries—completely circumscribed by the larger and harsher reality of the general park and its general public—was a slight and delicate miracle, an indulgence granted only by the momentary distractions and restraining powers of marijuana, booze, parents, and rock music. That freedom is an illusion could have no better example than the grove; a matter of seconds (the amount of time that it might take, say, for neural impulses to travel from brain to arm and manifest themselves in movement and violence) was all that separated indulgence from destruction.

Wishing to fool myself no longer, I stopped thinking

and focused on the street. Keith drove slowly, turned left and right, and right yet again—had the car been skates on ice we would have drawn grand, rough arabesques. But then we stopped before an apartment complex on the opposite side of campus from my house. We went in and stripped and lay on the bed—just a mattress on the floor, piled with pillows and layered with plain white sheets and a green wool army surplus blanket. The rest of the studio was furnished with a kitchen table that also served as a desk, two wooden chairs, one tattered over-stuffed chair, its wide arms piled with books, a black-and-white TV, and a brown vinyl beanbag chair. We made love that time, and when we were done, I felt empty and drained of energy. I sat up against the wall and sighed. Keith lit a cigarette and sat up beside me, leaning forward for a moment to flick on the TV. He turned the sound down low and looked over at me.

"I like the way you look," he said.

I shrugged my shoulders. "Thanks."

"No, I'm serious," he said. "You've got the look of a country boy—the real look. It's your plaid shirt, your boots, the way you carry yourself. I like it."

I smiled. "Rugged?"

"Yeah, sure, why not . . . rugged," he said. "And I like your green eyes . . ."

He was bugging me already. "Oh," I said flatly. He sat back and stared at the TV. I couldn't think of anything to say. I liked the way *he* looked, too, but I couldn't say anything about it, not then, not in that dreary place. I was dissatisfied, though the mood was imprecise. So I nestled down into the pillows and stared at the TV.

At length he said, "You know, it's true that I've never

been to the grove before. I've known about it for a long time, but there's always those teenage kids in the parking lot, and you don't know what might . . ."

I frowned.

He turned his palms up, then lit another cigarette and remained silent for a moment. I was wondering, questioning, and then I asked, "What do you do then, if you don't go to the grove?"

"I mostly go to the city on weekends," he answered. "You know, to the baths and bars," he went on. "And they've got fabulous discos. You can dance until morning. Don't you ever go?"

I shook my head and shrugged my shoulders and made a face of boredom. He was convinced of my disinterest, though the fact was I was more than interested, but embarrassed by my lack of experience.

"Well, I'm probably going to move down there before very long," he said. "I can't think of any really good reason to stay up here. The college is not all that great."

I said nothing. I was irritated at what I took to be a veiled criticism of my life, and I was disturbed by my apprehensions about San Francisco, apprehensions that I did not understand but that had something to do with a suspicion that there was, somewhere, a place where it might be easier.

But I wouldn't think of it, not then.

He looked at me, softly, and said, "What are you doing tomorrow?"

"What?" I said, pretending to have fallen nearly asleep, stalling long enough to imagine some excuse.

"Would you like to do something tomorrow?" he asked.

"Oh, well, I have classes and an appointment and then I promised to see some people." I wasn't convincing. Or perhaps I was, if he could read between the lines.

"Oh," he said. Then, "Here, let me give you my number." He got up and scrawled his phone number on a scrap of paper and handed it to me.

"Thanks," I said as I got up and started to dress. "I'll call you next week, maybe?"

He smiled and nodded, and I put the piece of paper in my pocket. I could see disappointment in his eyes, but at that moment I felt only that this was not the path I intended ever to take. To find a lover in the shrubs in the middle of the night—the idea filled me with despair. For I envisioned—as the perfect way to meet a lover, not a trick—a chance encounter at the grocery or while waiting in line for a movie. Earlier that evening just such an encounter had occurred, when at the party that handsome young man had introduced himself as Stephen. And as I walked home across the silent midnight expanse of campus, I was torn between the recent pleasure of Keith and the perfect hope for Stephen.

I got home and went inside. I took off my jeans and saw they were dusty. I brushed them out and hung them up. Just before I went to bed, I took Keith's phone number and put it in the drawer of my bureau. Then I lay down, closed my eyes, and tried to remember if Stephen had said anything to me. But my memory of the party was clouded and distorted.

I lay there, nowhere near sleep, and I imagined what life might be like had I chosen some other college, or had

I chosen to stay in the hometown, perhaps to pump gas or to box groceries. But that tiny town had had so little to offer—it was nothing more than the dying outpost of an old river economy now as abandoned and forgotten as the steamboats and mule trains upon which it had once depended. The passage of gold from the hills to the cities had created scores of busy hamlets along the rivers and passes, but, long since, the gold had gone and the glory with it. What remained in those towns (which were hometowns to so very many of us) were the stately homes, the wide avenues lined with maples and elms, the central towers of stone courthouses and city halls, examples of a variety of architectural styles: Italianate, Edwardian, Queen Anne, Neoclassic. There had been no choice, truly. Those towns were dying precisely because their young people were always moving away—livings had to be made. I thought of those last years in high school, before I left for this other country town and its campus of the state college (its only true lifeblood aside from agriculture). I remembered how my grandfather used to shuffle around his mobile home, watering the roses, the tiny blue spruce, the patch of marigolds and petunias. I remembered how in the heat of summer we would lie awake, my sister and I, and try to guess the number of railroad cars in a train by counting the number of even-rhythmed ba-thumps. I pictured quail, ponies, manzanita bushes, and oak trees. I remembered how plain it all had seemed, how eager I had been to get away to college. I thought of my family, fixed in my mind as they were when I had left—how my mother had a weekly appointment every Saturday afternoon at the beauty parlor—she'd come home with her hair piled up and spend the night half-propped up in bed so as not to ruin the "height" before church. She spent my childhood either dieting or eating, fluctuating between plumpness and thinness, back and forth. I remembered how she used to stand at the ironing board and sprinkle starch and water out of a Coca-Cola bottle onto my stepfather's white shirts; she'd roll them up then and stick them in the freezer. Then, later, after they were frozen, she'd turn the record player on, put on calypso music or Harry Belafonte and iron those frozen shirts. Twice a year she would pack a large wardrobe full of her most elegant dresses, gloves, hats, heels, and her one fur, and off she would go in the train with my rich aunt to San Francisco. She always spoke of San Francisco's shopping with a far-away look in her eye: "Why, all the ladies wear hats and gloves to do their buying!" And when she'd come back, she'd bring my sister and me some small tourist item. One year I received a miniature wind-up cable car that I would roll across the porch. I thought of my stepfather, of how fat he had been, how his big belly had hung over his belt. He'd had a large nose—his French descent, he always said—which he would use to caricature Jews: "You guess vhat I iss!" he'd say to a crowd of his friends. They'd all shriek and hoo-ha and say "Shush! You shouldn't!" He never allowed me to go directly home after grade school. I had to stop by his office and wait for him to go home, for I was not trusted to be home alone, and my mother worked longer than he. So I sat there— for years it must have been—and swung my legs back and forth and watched him sit and study the Bible. Once, as I sat there, he produced a photograph of the Beatles from his desk drawer and demanded: "Is this yours?" I said that it was, one of my friends had given it to me and I'd left it on my dresser at home. "They're sinful!" he told me. "That long hair!" I remembered my sister's extensive collection of photos and magazine articles about Julie Andrews, culled from years of combing movie magazines, and *LOOK*, and newspapers. My sister had been thin and nervous, which my mother explained was the result of my sister's brilliance. The school counselor had tested her and found her to be a genius! The genius stayed in her room most of the time watching old movies on TV: *Sylvia Scarlett, Charade, It Happened One Night, In the Good Old Summertime, Meet Me in St. Louis, The Haunting of Hill House.* I loved her dearly for her cinematic preferences. To me it betrayed the finest taste of anyone around, so superior was it to that of the other townsfolk who preferred simple programs like "Route 66" or the "Lawrence Welk Show." I remembered the details of that old river town, its cobblestone sidewalks and Old West false fronts downtown. I remembered how stupid and vicious most of the other kids had been in that town, so straight and smug. I had never fit in. I remembered how I used to stand beside the river below our house and look across at the city river park, its parking lot full of teenagers whose loud music I could hear as it carried across the water. I would shelter myself beside the big bent sycamore and simply stare at those other kids. I'd wonder if I would ever be like them, but by the time I was old enough to realize that I would not, I had lost the desire. I'd had but one hope then—to escape that town to college. It was a hope that had been fulfilled, for as I lay there remembering and thinking, unable to sleep for my restlessness over Stephen and Keith, I was living amidst the very real moments of the life about which I had so determinedly fantasized: to escape to college.

When I next saw Stephen he was standing at the foot of the stairs in my neighbor's entry hall. He was dressed for a run and was speaking to someone at the head of the stairs whom I did not know. Being only an acquaintance of my new neighbor and hostess, I said nothing. He turned and ran down the porch steps and into the street without seeing me.

My neighbor, Alison Johnson, was one of the new lecturers in anthropology. She was so young that she mingled more easily with students than with faculty, and it happened that the house she rented was in the midst of the student ghetto, next door to the large house in which I had my room.

We had met only the week before, at the start of the term, while she sat on her front porch smoking one late afternoon. I had introduced myself, and I think that she had taken me in with a glance; perhaps it was her anthropological training that endowed her with insight. In any event, she had invited me for dinner, and I was arriving for our first drink when I saw that perfect young man bounding out the door.

Now, Professor Johnson enjoyed a drink. I discovered she had learned to put it away while doing fieldwork in central Mexico, for it had been, as she put it, as "boring as hell down there," passing the days with pregnant women and squawking chickens. But that evening I had little interest in discussions of her research, because I was preoccupied with the vision of Stephen I had witnessed earlier. When she had tippled sufficiently during the cocktail hour, I interrupted her monologue on Oaxacan weaving to venture a question about Stephen. How did she know him?

"Oh, he lives down the street, for heaven's sake. He's

my best friend Dale's cousin. She's upstairs writing her dissertation." She swallowed her drink and studied the ice cubes for a long moment. "Why?"

I shrugged my shoulders as though it didn't matter. Of course it mattered a great deal. I could think of nothing else, and I was poised on the edge of my chair in anticipation of whatever Professor Johnson was about to say.

But she said nothing. She kept studying her ice cubes, until I broke down and asked, "Do you know him very well?"

She looked up at me, grinned, reached over to the table beside her to light a cigarette. She took a long draw on it, all the while keeping an eye fixed on me. I was terrified by her melodrama, and then she said, "No, he's not."

I laughed and loved her for that. We had dinner then, crêpes stuffed with marinated artichoke hearts and mushrooms. We drank Napa Valley wine and talked about nothing of importance. She seemed to accept my curiosity.

I kept thinking about Stephen and I wondered: Could I cultivate at least a friendship? But Alison had shaken her head briefly at me when she had said "No, he's not." And so I already knew the rejoinder to my own question: What good would it do to go after a straight guy?

But it had begun. There was a sudden point after dinner, after I had watched Professor Johnson drink three more cocktails and smoke seven cigarettes, after I had left and walked to the park, when I was feeling the heat of a stranger's body against my own, that the downward spiral began, when the whole thing was put into motion, and I was driven not to be lonely. Surely there was a way; there had to be. I clung to my hope like a nun to her faith—when life has little to offer, we embrace whatever we have, as small or as weary as it may be. It was as though my first chance at love was Stephen, and it was as if Stephen was my only chance. There would be no one else.

And what did I remember of Keith? His phone number fell beneath my gaze each time I retrieved a pair of socks from the bureau, but it represented nothing more than a potential vent for some possible future need—physical, someone to talk to, a favor perhaps.

Later that night, as I returned from the park, walking fast along that broad, tree-lined avenue, I stopped just short of going into my house and took three deep breaths. It wasn't very late, actually, for a Friday, and I listened as a cold autumn breeze brushed leaves along the sidewalk. A dog barked in the next block. Across the street a screen door flapped in the breeze, banged shut with a thud, then swung wide again, its hinges creaking. It was very dark. I looked up at the house, a square shadow against the night sky. There was only one light shining, from Ann's window. Someone had even put out the porch light, so I felt my way up the front steps as if I were blind.

What draws one man to another in the gathering dusk of an autumn evening? I asked myself as I stumbled up those stairs. Is it the need to cling to summer's fading warmth through the warmth of another, to abandon the loneliness of long, lazy days?

There was something about the season, I told myself. I had always regarded autumn as *my* time of the year. It evoked warm emotions and images of fires, piles of leaves, pumpkin pies, new classes, a resurrection of busy habits that held the promise of security, of family. Autumn was the only time of year we could expect thunderstorms, the imposing rumble and shocking flashes creating a hellish world in place of the dreary evenness of country life. And in college, autumn was all: early darkness, seminars, new ideas, a ruckus of plans and hopes.

I stood in the dark entry hall of the house and felt the richness of the wood panels, the depth of roommates sleeping, no sound whatsoever. The carpet seemed thick and luxurious. The tiles were cool and Mediterranean. The house was suddenly rather grand and palatial.

I went upstairs and knocked on Ann's door. She was reading, but she put her book down and asked me to come in. Ann was the only confidant I had. She knew nearly everything there was to know about me, though I hid the details of what took place between men in the grove. With her blond page-boy hair and pale, slightly golden skin, Ann evoked images of happy Swedes, but this appearance was contradicted by her personality—a vein of wisdom bound her to earth, just short of melancholy. She smiled and patted the bedside. I sat down and leaned my head against the wall in that manner suggesting wistful abandon, behavior that was as much for effect as it was an accurate reflection of my mood.

"Oh, my, what is it?" she asked.

"His name is Stephen. He wears red running shorts, and he lives at the end of the block." Without intending to, I sighed, a betrayal of very real melodrama, then sat up straight to compensate.

"This isn't going to be one of those hope-to-catch-a-glance sort of things, is it?" asked Ann as she closed the book for good and laid it on the bedside table.

"I've never thought about anything like that," I said, and I raised my eyebrows as proof.

Which was partly true. A bland pessimism had always led me along the path of doubt. To befriend someone like Stephen or to sleep with a man like that—well, it was nigh unto impossible. For a few moments I said nothing, and Ann sat still, her hand drawing circles on the coverlet. She had that manner so perfected by practitioners of the analytic sciences, the long silence by which the therapist evokes both trust and discussion. Finally I sat up and shook my head, as though in dismissal. Ann did not smile, but she asked, "How are you going to do it? Do you have a plan?"

I leaned against the wall and thought her question rather queer. But then I surrendered myself to the fantasy. "I'm not sure," I said. "But I know it must be subtle. I can't just make a pass at him or make some blatant proposition. It should be gradual, a friendship first, then conversation, then more talking I suppose . . ."

She shook her head and said, "Don't do it. Leave it alone."

I nodded and left. Usually we might have argued, or I might have persuaded her to listen to me, to entertain whatever idea we were debating, to share and make suggestions. But the certainty of her warning—the simple strength of the tone of her voice—angered me. I wanted no discouragement, and like a youngster intent on having candy long after the candy store has been passed, when the family is already in the car and back on the highway, I nursed my anger and shadowed my face and went to my room and closed the door.

I got into bed and lay there thinking about Stephen's face, picturing it again and again, the blue-green eyes, or were they grey? I thought about the way he had run so vigorously into the street, not even seeing me.

I rolled onto my side and switched on the reading light. I picked up my copy of Thoreau and tried to read myself to sleep. Eventually I set the book back down and put out the light.

Soon it began to rain, and the muffled sound of distant thunder lulled me to sleep. Sometime in the middle of the night, the rain stopped suddenly. The broken rhythm wakened me, and for a moment I lay still, not remembering where I was. I turned over and felt that my arm was numb, and I sat up and shook it back and forth gently. It tingled, and I relaxed—it wasn't paralyzed after all. Then the gentle patter resumed at the window, and I rested my head against the pillow, my heart suddenly full of courage: I would ask Stephen to go running with me the next day.

Later in the morning I drank coffee and looked at the headlines in the paper and drummed up the nerve to walk down the street to look for Stephen. Around noon the rain stopped and the sky cleared, revealing a pale blue canopy through which moved a very bright and very hot sun. The heat on the damp sidewalks brought steam rising from the concrete, and I walked through ankle-deep wisps of fog.

Just as I had hoped, there he was, sitting on the front steps, dressed for classes and preparing to go. "Stephen!" I called out, and he stood and walked over to me. The heavy leather satchel that he carried over his shoulder swayed against him. "We met at the party," I explained to his puzzled expression, and he laughed, nodding his head. "Alison says you might want a running partner," I lied.

He smiled and said, "Sure, later today? This afternoon?"

From that moment we became friends. It began with an afternoon run, proceeded with cycling through the park, long walks, late-night dancing, evening talks on front porches. We ran every day that fall, without exception. Through the park we raced along, side by side, conversing in breathless banter. The sight of our two sweaty bodies became familiar to our friends—he in his red running shorts and white tank top, I in my navy-and-white-striped shorts and black T-shirt. In the park we dodged golden branches and tall dry grasses. We learned about each other:

Stephen was the son of a municipal engineer, had been born in Oklahoma and raised on Air Force bases around the country—Maryland, Texas, California. His family settled finally in Berkeley, where he graduated from high school. He was a twenty-three-year-old Capricorn and, by baptism only, Episcopalian—"although that's not an adjective," he corrected himself. "Our priest when I was in the fifth grade instructed us that the word 'Episcopalian' could be a noun only, and not a very good one at that. It was years before I understood what he meant, and now I can't forget it." He studied foreign languages and world history, but his goal was either to go to medical school or, as he joked, to become the gigolo of a rich woman.

He took inordinate pride in his face and in his physique, though he regarded them as separate entities requiring individual attention. For his physique he ran, performed scores of sit-ups each morning before showering and each evening just before going to bed, and occasionally lifted weights. For his face he took just a bit of sun, and before doing his evening sit-ups he sat before the mirror and screwed his face up in a series of toning exercises for precisely twelve minutes.

Certain of these physical preoccupations I took as indicators of possible latent homosexuality, for I had yet to learn about the inescapable vanity of all men. He exuded enthusiasm, loved Mozart and backgammon, and was rarely given to brooding or inner reflection. He woke always eager to "get going" and retired reluctantly.

Days and weeks passed. One night we sat beside the dance floor of a discotheque and admired the dancers. "And what do you think of her?" he asked as he inclined his head in the direction of two plump blondes, one black girl, and one buxom brunette.

"I take it you mean the one with the tits," I said.

He grimaced. "Yeah, her. What do you think?"

"She probably has chronic back pain," I said.

But he shook his head. "No, she's fine."

I had been through this sort of commentary before. I merely rolled my eyes.

"I'm going to meet her," he announced, which surprised me. And off he went across the dance floor, winding his way through twisting limbs and flashing lights like an explorer penetrating a jungle. I sat and observed their interaction: She turned and smiled at him, expectantly. He smiled—wryly, with the corner of his mouth only—and gestured with his hand to the dance floor. She nodded and whispered into his ear. They laughed and stepped onto the dance floor, joining the crowd rendered freakish by the blinding strobes of blue, red, green, and white. *The natives are restless tonight,* I told myself. *These tribal ceremonies are most curious. Shall we make note of how foolishly they behave? Surely this is not human nature?*

But I could see them too clearly, quite. I could see her boobs bouncing around and his tight little round ass rotating. She tossed her head and shook out a full mane of hair. I groaned. I stopped drinking beer and ordered a Sidecar, then another, a salute to Auntie Mame, to the frivolity of life.

I left the disco and walked the streets, angry and befuddled, disgusted. I loved him, but there was nothing doing. What could I do? Did it make any difference? I sat in the square downtown and stared at the intersection before me, three corners—a Taco Bell, a Jack-in-the-Box, and a service station. I studied the plastic signs and disparaged the poor taste of heterosexual life. I understood what it was that drove people to hurl themselves from bridges or to stick their heads into ovens after watching something on TV. Why should one go on living in a world of breasts and plastic?

As I sat staring into the street and gathering my mantle of bitterness about me, a group of Chicanos gathered to admire an orange automobile that appeared to be half Chevy Vega and half Camaro. Long chrome pipes protruded here, there, and everywhere, suggesting a mobile men's room. The group grew larger. There were a half-dozen teenage guys and three or four Latino chicks. The driver gunned the motor and revved it up. The group cheered. Then they all climbed in and tore away in a cloud of blue smoke.

I smiled and stood up, turned to walk home. I was glad that the young Mexican was proud of his car. I hoped that they all had a fine party somewhere. I went back to the house—now deathly quiet in the middle of the night—and went to bed.

I continued to spend as much time with him as I could. I studied every move and every gesture, every facial expression and tone of voice. When we could not be together, I hurried to accomplish neglected errands. Of course there were classes to attend and books to read— life *did* go on. But sometimes I sat for hours on the front porch alone, thinking of nothing but the stretch of his thighs as he ran or the way he leaned forward after running to rest his palms against his knees, his lungs gasping for air, his back heaving. I suspected I had found escape—a man—and though we had not touched as lovers, I was blind to any discussion to the contrary. For I was his lover in my heart, and like contemplatives who vow silence and endure endless vigils of reverence, so I experienced pleasure in denial. I spoke to him in nothing but metaphors and parables:

"When I was thirteen," I told him, "our family made a pilgrimage to the Holy Land. We stopped in Athens on the way, and one day my folks decided to visit the Acropolis. I pleaded fatigue and remained at the hotel. An office building was being erected across the street, and I wanted only to sit at the window and stare at the burly Greek workers . . ."

Or I told him:

"The real reason I study anthropology is because as a child we had a constant stream of missionaries through our home. They brought slides of vast hordes of near-naked Negroes and told tales of heathen rites deep in the heart of the Congo . . . and because I like Professor Johnson."

Or, one evening I said:

"I cannot stop rereading *To the Lighthouse*. I'm absolutely caught by the drama of it all. Listen to this passage . . ." And there I quoted a long, rambling scene from the book, as Stephen sat silently smiling.

Stephen took it all in with mild amusement, indulgence perhaps. "But what can I say?" he asked me one night. "I don't read that much. I don't have your mind."

I blushed and said nothing. I was ashamed at having misrepresented myself intellectually. I wasn't brilliant, nor witty. I felt I was something of a sham, but when I had neither breasts nor pussy to offer, I felt I needed to serve up something for his consumption.

One day we stood beside the swimming pond in the public park, and Stephen interrupted me in the middle of a pompous and phony discourse on the empire of the Ostrogoths to say:

"Something's wrong."

The city had dammed the creek at that point and constructed concrete walls about the shore. The dam held back the fresh mountain stream and created a deep, cold pool. The water was natural and soft, icy and clear. Children waded, and brave blond boys dove in, emerging with pink flesh and goose pimples.

"I know," I said—though "wrong" was not the word I would have chosen. I might have said "unusual," or "curious," or "unclear."

Stephen steered us towards a bench away from the water, beneath the canopy of an oak, and we sat. The gnarled branches were clearly visible, the tree's leaves fully stripped and spread around the tree like a fallen skirt.

"It has nothing to do with anything I can name," he started, "but for some damn reason I can't stop thinking about what's happening here."

Is this coyness genuine? I asked myself. Nothing to do with anything he could name? Could name! Two little boys dodged around us, chasing each other in circles with sticks. Their mother stood to the side at some distance and pleaded with them to behave. One little boy fell and scraped his knee. At his instant outburst of tears and wails, his brother whacked him with his stick and laughed victoriously. Their mother scolded them.

"Spell it out," I said. For a brief moment I was frightened. What was he going to say? Would there be anger? Would there be cruelty? Could I control myself? (For the truth is, certain men can make other men feel like children.)

"No," said Stephen. "You tell me."

Suddenly I was excited at the prospect of confessing what I felt. Let's be done with it once and for all, I told myself. I frowned in order to give weight to my upcoming words, although I was amused to see that the mother of the two brats had turned the mean one over her knee and was spanking him with satisfying vigor.

"Enough cat and mouse," I said. A tone of exasperation and a heavy, affected sigh. A wistful sidelong glance. Silence stretching like a punctuation mark. "I'm in love with you, all right?" And oh, the thousand subtle, unconscious, unintended, and unexpected meanings in the tagging-on of the question "all right?"

"You mean you think I'm gay?"

"Goddammit," I said, but then stopped. Dusk was coming on fast, and just as I spoke, the iron park lights flashed on, casting long stripes of rippling light on the water. I stalled for some time and feigned calm. "It's not that simple," I went on. I watched the stripes of light undulate, then break. I lied: "No, I haven't thought of it one way or the other. Maybe I'd hoped, but . . ." He was frowning. I went on, "I don't know what to expect of you. Nothing, I guess." It was hardly a brilliant confession. And from the confused expression on his face, I realized he hadn't understood me.

We kept a period of silence. Shadows lengthened in the twilight. A chill breeze stirred the crisp leaves. The surface of the water was blacker, the stripes of light more steady. That silence communicated nothing. Unlike some silences, which hold fury or hurt or deep reverence, that silence was meaningless.

At length he said, "Guys always tell me that."

I breathed. "What? Oh, so . . . guys are always telling you what?"

He shrugged his shoulders, as if to dismiss the remark, then asked, "What is it about me, anyway?" There was innocence in his tone—and vulnerability.

I shrugged my shoulders. "You're beautiful," I answered.

"Why don't you make a pass at me?"

"Do you want me to?" I asked.

"Do you want to make love to me?" he asked.

"Yes, but do you?"

"No, but why haven't you tried?"

"What are you saying?" I asked. What was his game? "I don't understand. After this tension I tell you I love you and you want to know why I don't grab you? Even as you tell me that you don't want it?"

"Yes, why not?"

"Are you interested?" I asked.

"No!" he protested.

"So don't play this game with me," I said. I looked down at my feet, measured the distance between them, stepped on a dry leaf, looked back up, looked at Stephen's hand on the bench, and restrained myself from caressing it. "You don't know how this feels," I said.

He looked at me and shook his head. "No, I understand that people are cruel, but I'm not interested in men. Even the ones who I can see are beautiful don't do it, not like the beauty of women. I crave their softness. I've tried, you know. I've sat and stared at guys and tried to imagine the feel of their muscles, the shape of a man's body in my hands. But I don't get any further than that."

There was almost anguish in his voice. I was astonished and moved. For the longest moment I held another silence and listened to that precious trace of anguish reverberate in my mind. It was an unintentional disclosure of exceptional sensitivity. It seemed a gift.

But then his hand was on mine. I looked down at the bench, at our two hands, his on mine, mine under his. I panicked as I sat immobile and stared at our hands. They were still. And then his hand moved, closed, grasped mine warmly. His hand left mine and touched my thigh. I moved and looked at his face: innocence, coyness, deviltry. I looked at his neck: the pulse was obvious, throbbing the length of that flesh.

We left the park and went to his rooms, upstairs at his house. My heart raced too fast and I discovered a shadowed philosophy: One passion is just like another. We were ghosts that night—that evening only—hovering above the fire and looking down at the natives beating drums, chanting, leading lives wholly removed from the realms of vapors and spirits.

I went home afterward, to my own single bed, and nothing in the house had changed. Next morning, the news was as always. Later the next afternoon, I received a letter from my grandmother that detailed the mundanities of life at home: the chickens were dying of "chicken cancer"; the woodpile had a pack of rats; my mother was voted president of the Toastmistress Club; Jerry and Frieda were married the week before; Uncle Chuck got a promotion; Betty and Quincy were in their fourth month driving around the country in their RV.

But from that point we knew where we stood, and as the semester moved us further from autumn nights and closer to the twinkling lights of Christmas, we were side by side in a quiet understanding. "What is it with you two?" Ann asked repeatedly. "Is there something you're not telling me?" I always shook my head and shrugged my shoulders, which infuriated her. Alison also pressed for details, but there were none I wished to report. I was mystified by this confusion and wondered why others could not simply accept what they saw.

But I, too, was confused, for although this new and intimate friendship held my loneliness at bay, still I longed for deeper association. Our friendly intimacy opened great caverns of bewilderment within me—pale thoughts about what it meant to be homosexual, curiosity about that city of men in San Francisco, and wavering doubts about the possibility of ever escaping this thing, this yearning about which I had always felt too much and done too little.

I wanted the yearning to go away, and the sadness, too, for these had always attended my life without relief. I had hoped that sex with Stephen would relieve these emotions—this ceaseless mood—but it was useless.

As the semester finished, Stephen announced that he was going to move back to Berkeley to live with his family for a while. He would try to transfer to the university there. I accepted the news with a smile and said nothing. I knew that I would stay on and read late into the night, perhaps write a letter or two to him in Berkeley. And so, as quickly as we had come together, we were separated. He moved just after Christmas, and my life returned to the gentler rhythms I had known before. I embraced hope once again and lingered through January, a dead month when the college was not in session. I wasted days in my room, curled up in bed watching television and reading. That month I read John Hawkes and May Sarton and a handful of scripts. In late afternoons I walked through the park to the grove, which in winter became a complicated world of tangled vines stripped of leaves, the towering forest dark and dripping, the paths muddy.

Men still knelt to perform their duty, still bent themselves across damp logs and mossy tree stumps. And everywhere was the muted music of mist collecting in the trees and dripping.

Six months later I awoke on a hot Saturday morning in summer, and after wiping the sweat from my face, sat on the front steps and thought. I felt that my life was piling up against a wall of loneliness and frustration. Stephen had gone back to Berkeley, though I had had one short postcard from him, from Mexico, saying nothing but that Mexico was beautiful and he would be back in Berkeley soon. There was no date and no legible postmark. Ann was at home in Oakland. My professors were on sabbatical or vacation. And the prospect of more study filled me with a sense of purposelessness, as if the rigors of academia were nothing more than self-indulgence.

At that time of year, the town was completely deserted, as empty as any college town in summer. In the central district surrounding campus, great houses, which overflowed with bustle and excitement during the academic year, now sat empty, or nearly empty. Sometimes a lone student attending summer session remained; or someone who lacked any other retreat during summer break stayed on, no family. On campus, nothing moved in the afternoons but the heavy green leaves of the oaks and sycamores, the few summer students having left shortly after lunch, their early classes dismissed for the day. Inside the concrete and brick library some students and faculty slouched in soft chairs or slumped over long tables, the soft whistle of air-conditioning the only sound. Long tinted windows shielded the glaring afternoon sun and created an interior that seemed, in its gloom and chill, like a refrigerator. When one left the building and passed through heavy glass doors, an exchange of chilly pressurized air, and hot, damp summer rushed past one's ears, and then, once outside, only the deep hum of the air-conditioning units atop the building could be heard. I walked toward the heart of campus and saw that the student union was deserted, the creek dry, the stillness broken only by the sudden whir of a passing bicyclist, the distant sound of a car horn, or the somber tolling of the campanile issuing across the vast, empty lawns and plazas.

Long, dark halls of other buildings were cool and vacant. With lights out and bulletin boards empty they resembled something plain yet extraordinary, like fallout shelters or abandoned church houses. It seemed austere and frightening as I went walking by myself across campus and through those deserted halls. Every door I opened revealed empty, silent rooms or lecture halls descending into darkness. I stepped into one and called out, my voice echoing in a way the biology professor's never had. I stood beside the dry creek or at the concrete amphitheater and watched traffic through the trees. I wandered off campus and into town, ate ice cream, and strolled aimlessly. Once, I saw my classics professor, but we spoke only briefly, having nothing, really, to say. I shrugged my shoulders and walked away.

Late one evening I tried to phone Stephen, but there was no answer. I phoned Ann in Oakland and told her that the town was deserted and I was lonely. "Of course it is and so you are," she agreed. "It's time for you to move your butt."

I grunted and hung up and went out on the porch. The temperature had dropped somewhat, yet the evening was sultry. I thought about the grove, but I couldn't go.

The next night—and the rest that summer—I walked the town in utter silence. I avoided the grove with its thin promise of momentary pleasure—I'd had enough and longed for too much. Instead I would simply walk the town, late into the night. I would stand on a corner or in the square downtown and watch teenagers get drunk. Lovers—young and straight—strolled arm in arm, stopped for momentary kisses, then moved on. Pale streetlights cast illuminated swaths through which passed old men leaning on canes, retired farmers and their wives, delinquent brats, and unleashed dogs. These nightly scenes made life remarkably lonely, in the way it feels to stand at the edge of a cliff or in an empty cathedral.

I was free in my isolation to pursue the distractions that most suited me—reading late into the night, movies (I enjoyed sitting alone very near the screen), old television programs, the piano. For weeks I retreated into a world of paperback novels. I chose to read Nazi spy novels, Emerson, and Thoreau. My tastes were indiscriminate and eclectic, so long as the book was a paperback and could be carried in my hip pocket. Then, sitting in the shade after a walk or stripping off my shirt to sun myself by the dry creekbed, I could handily grab whatever book offered greatest escape that day and lose myself for hours.

But the joys of the town ceased to instill happiness as they once had. The deep woods of the park suddenly seemed thick and infested with disagreeable creatures. The quaint shops and small houses became junky and rickety symbols of the poverty of rural life. And the amiable, congenial townsfolk—once so honest and plain— were ignorant, intolerable hicks. I became one of those people the townsfolk complained about, a lazy college student walking the streets with nothing to do but frown and criticize, read and get drunk. Groups of ancient, aging men and women blocked my path as I walked in the evening. The sun was relentless.

As another autumn approached I awoke one morning and told myself I must move away, to Berkeley. Withdrawal from the university was amazingly easy—once the decision was made—a simple matter of filling out forms. In an hour I was free of the institution and culture that had once seemed my lifeblood. The secular world became a salvation, and as I took those final walks beneath elms and cedars just beginning to brown in late summer, I remembered how it had felt to be on summer vacation in high school, full of the freedom and possibility I was suddenly feeling once again.

I didn't know what I would do, but I called Stephen and told him I was coming. "It's about time," he said. "You can stay at my friend Clem's place. He's in Mexico until November, and I have the keys." Ann screamed the same sentence to me over the phone: "It's about time! When will you get here?"

And in the manner of a traveler I hastened to pack.

I gave away most of my things. I didn't want that junk anymore. I left much of it for the incoming household, a rowdy bunch of sophomores and juniors already descending on the place as I hurried to settle my bank accounts, my memberships, my packing and throwing away.

It was warm and hazy the day I left. The trees were shedding leaves in constant streams. Students were arriving in cars and vans. Argyle sweaters were being placed on display in the windows downtown. I drove away from it all, and it was an hour later, as I passed through a sleepy, sun-baked hamlet and stopped to buy a soda, that I remembered how dearly I used to love that town in autumn.

3

The drive was hot and monotonous through those dull flat towns, each nothing more than a series of service stations, churches, and roadside cafes with blinking lights. Passing through one of those towns was like struggling to emerge from amnesia: something stirred recognition but then faded. After a town, one would pass into the countryside once again, the road flanked by orchards of almonds, and peaches, and plums; walnuts gave way to corn and tomatoes; chicken farms bordered dairy farms. Their musty smells filled the car, swirled in through the vents and whistled out the windows. At one point—for several miles—the road was elevated above dank acres of rice fields planted in grand jigsaws punctuated by levees. The earth stretched away from the causeway in sea-green mud. Wild grasses pricked the dull surface, which under the heat of the sun gave off an acrid humidity so suffocating that one thought of jungles and wars. The rice fields yielded finally to many canals crossed by tiny, intricate iron bridges, and as the state highway twisted, my hands busied themselves rotating the wheel, tuning the radio, and adjusting the visor against the shifting sun.

When I arrived in Berkeley, fog was rolling in, a sight so new and foreign I had to stop the car to study it. A long grey finger of mist pointed its way across San Francisco Bay, inched its way into west Berkeley and on up into the hills. The sudden sight of a natural event so dramatic filled me with a sense of apprehension. What was I doing? Why had I left that town? As I edged the car back onto the freeway I felt bereft for a moment, as though to leave my known world behind to face a jungle of aliens was perhaps not the best choice.

Following the directions he had given me, I drove straight to Stephen's family's house, a great stone mansion nestled amidst a stand of eucalyptus in the Berkeley hills. Vines of ivy climbed the walls and trailed down the hill and clung like spiderwebs to trees. Long, small-paned windows punctuated the imposing facade, and a grand, intricately carved oak door faced me as I lifted the iron knocker and pounded. I waited there for a moment and took a chill. The damp breeze christened the ivy with mist. There was no sound but that of branches creaking in the breeze and then, suddenly, footsteps falling heavy and fast behind the door.

It opened, and Stephen hugged me and asked me in. I looked around me: an immense redwood drawing room; an interior garden of blue orchids, ferns, azaleas, and jasmine.

"How the hell are you?" Stephen asked as he steered me to a simple Shaker bench.

I told him about the drive, about how strange the fog had seemed to me as I'd entered town.

"Oh, god, yes," he said, "the fog gets everybody going. It's really wonderful, though. Eventually you get to love it."

I looked out the window at it, but it had receded somewhat. I suggested we go out and get something to eat.

"I can't believe you're here!" he declared, reaching out to pat my arm as if to confirm my presence. "Let me get the keys to Clem's place, and then we'll go."

He went upstairs, and I studied a tapestry over the fireplace, a medieval hunting scene. Stephen returned and handed me the keys. "Here they are. Clem's gone to Mexico until around Christmas, so you can use the place till then."

"Who is he?" I asked as we walked out of the house and down to the street.

"One of my best friends from high school. Clem's sort of like a leftover hippie, except of course he's way too young," Stephen explained. I frowned. He went on, "He went to Mexico with a small group of people who follow this sort of psychiatrist-guru, but they have to go to Mexico to do their psychedelic drug workshops. So right now he's probably up on a mountain somewhere in the Yucatan seeing visions of Quetzalcoatl or something."

I nodded, then realized that Stephen was being humorous. So I laughed. We drove down steep streets, and again everything was new and, this time, refreshing. I noticed everything—the narrow streets, the dense trees, the kooks on street corners, the European way the streets split and twisted through rows of mansions.

"I can't believe you're really here," he said again. "Turn left." We pulled up beside a coffee shop and went upstairs to a tiny restaurant. We sat on an outdoor deck and ate sandwiches. We could see the bay from there, and I noticed that the fog had pulled back even further.

"Does it do that all the time?" I asked. "It was foggy, and now it's clearing up."

He nodded. "Sometimes it can't make up its mind. Usually it just pours in, but once in a while it pulls back and sort of boils out there behind the Golden Gate Bridge." Stephen pointed, and I squinted.

"It looks rather threatening like that," I said as I saw what he meant. The fog was churning in great billows behind the bridge, but unmoving, as if held back somehow, by some invisible barrier.

"I just can't believe—," he started.

"But I am!" I cut him off. "And I really want to know what you've been doing since you left last winter. There weren't many letters or calls," I chastised him.

"Okay, okay, but it's a long story," he started.

"They all are," I said. "But go on."

"Well, after I got back here I started at Cal but dropped out because I couldn't concentrate. Things were happening, and sitting in class just wasn't to the point. So I got a job waiting tables and then fell in love with a fantastic woman named Meg who turned out to be a lesbian, so that was short-lived."

I shook my head and laughed. The sun had returned and was hot on the deck. "You fell in love with a lesbian . . ." I started, but didn't go on.

After a moment he went on, "In April, my friend

Mark and I went sailing on the bay in his catamaran, and we had some trouble with the rigging and the sail swung round, the boat veered hard to port, and then we barely missed ramming a huge yacht. Well, ahoys led to apologies and introductions and before we knew it we were on board the yacht for a party. It turned out it was the yacht of Anderson Stannage—the big shipping magnate, you know—and for the next five weeks we cruised up and down the Pacific Coast with them and went to Mexico—"

"So that's what that was all about," I interrupted, "because it was just after midterm exams that I got your postcard from Mexico, but you were so cryptic about it I hardly knew how you'd got there. I thought you'd just driven down for a couple weeks, that's all."

"Oh, no, it was about a month," he said. "When we were in Acapulco and Puerto Vallarta we just ate and drank—which is probably why my postcard was just babble—and get this—in Puerto Vallarta I was propositioned by the shipping magnate himself *and* his wife."

"Together?"

"No, individually! And then one night at a party in a mansion in Acapulco, another couple came up to me and asked if I'd go home with them for the night. She was a society matron and he was a professor emeritus! Of medieval history! He kept lapsing into Middle English all evening. I felt like I was living in an Edward Albee play.

"Anyway, after that, Berkeley seemed really dull, so I went to work at a punk-rock club down on University Avenue. But that didn't work out because I didn't look right, and I wouldn't change my haircut, so I quit and decided to just hang around the house all summer and do nothing." He sat back and stretched his arms above his head.

"Sounds okay," I said. I'd had no idea he'd done so much. We were quiet for a few minutes, the hot sun bearing down like a spotlight. For a moment I studied the fog again, still billowing behind the bridge. The bay was a deep emerald, as smooth as marble. There was quite a bit of chatter on the deck and frequent chimes of spoons on enamel coffee cups. I leaned back in my chair and yawned, just as Stephen leaned forward on his elbows and smiled.

"I'm so glad you're here," he said. "I think it'll be good for you. Things *are* pretty slow up there, especially if you're into guys."

So there it was, as simple as that. There wasn't even a hint of tension in his voice, nothing to betray even the slightest feeling. I reminded myself it had been nothing. I was silent.

"But what about you?" he asked. "What did you do? How do you feel about being here?"

"Oh, I don't know," I answered. "You know what I did—I finished my coursework and got out. The last few months were really a bore. I guess it was quite a strain, actually." I paused to collect my thoughts but found myself at a loss, with nothing to say. I wanted to feel something, but I was yet transitional, barely arrived. I had expected something different, though Stephen had never encouraged me. Our friendship was only that, and I felt a cleft as wide as a canyon between what I expected and what I knew.

"The summer was unbearably hot," I was saying, "with days when I woke up in a sweat and did nothing but sit on the porch and read. Sometimes I went to the library for the air-conditioning . . ." I kept talking, but my soul did not address Stephen's. Apparently there was nothing for them to say to each other. I imagined what I might say, how I might speak to him of passion, how I might bring profound meaning to something that truly did not exist. I wondered if I ought to say something to the effect that I thought he was possibly a latent homosexual (though I didn't) and that he should get his act together before leading someone else along (though he hadn't). I thought of how I might hold him responsible for my new life in Berkeley, how I might make myself dependent. I wondered if I could seduce him again somehow. But then, sitting in that hot sun, chattering mindlessly about summer, I felt suddenly, pathetically sorry for myself, for my loneliness, for my isolation, for my need. Why was there no one other than this straight boy? Why did the world seem to revolve around *him*—who was nothing, who did nothing, who gave no love, who was not of my kind? What was it going to take to find escape? Disappearance? Dreams? Was I disappearing by coming to Berkeley?

Stephen was speaking to me: "What kind of a job are you going to look for? What do you want to do?"

"What does an anthropology major do?" I asked. "I suppose I'll take what comes along and probably end up being a ribbon clerk somewhere. It doesn't really matter. That's not the point anyway."

"What is the point?" he asked, so directly and so quietly that I was stunned.

I didn't know. I was feeling lost, disoriented. And I could do nothing but sit mute, for in such moments of transition one loses all sense of purpose, and we tend, in purposelessness, to rely on immediate sensation, that of eyes, nose, ears, fingertips—and on the past, on memories as comfortable in their familiarity as a stack of pillows on one's bed, set precisely in the center of one's bedroom, cozily tucked away in a safe corner of the house. Our memories and knowledge and habits console us in the turbulence of change, and it was memory that wrapped its arms around me in soft embrace the moment Stephen directed me, by his question, to clearly define my purpose in life at that point. It was memory of a distant childhood which—at that moment, as I sat sipping coffee on a wooden deck and smelling the muted perfume of potted roses surrounding us on the railing wrapped around the deck—rose to awareness again—nearly an affliction of memory, had it not been so pleasantly comforting—only to make me shift in my chair and wonder at the fleeting images of a worn wood rocking horse, of an old Okie woman baby-sitter, of the sounds of football and cold whistling wind, of the way the light changed in the backyard when all the leaves had fallen from the trees and lay in magnificent crisp piles into which we dove and tunneled in frenzied silliness while Mother called from the kitchen window to "stop that this instant!" Even as I regarded these memories as evidence that surely I was safe in myself, I felt a foreboding that I was not at all safe. Because there were no touchstones around me on which the images could reflect, I felt adrift in this new world.

"I've met someone," he told me after the long silence. "Her name is Julie and we're going to get married." I smiled and said I was happy. Then there was nothing left to say, so we left the cafe and went to Clem's place, and Stephen handed me the keys.

Clem lived in an apartment over some stores. We examined the studio—small, cramped, someplace I would give closer attention to later—and afterward Stephen suggested we drive up to Grizzly Peak Boulevard to the vista point to watch the sun set on San Francisco. We drove high into the hills, and when we found the spot, we parked the car and walked to the edge of the hill. There were three or four other people there. One of them, a black man, was playing the guitar and humming to himself. Two or three others sat or stood and looked out across the bay to San Francisco and the bright pink clouds around the sun. The fog had retreated even farther and lay completely inert, nearly beyond sight. Stephen and I nodded and said hello to the people, but no one answered us. Eventually, when we had been sitting for a while, the black man offered us some bourbon and cigarettes. Stephen took some of the liquor, but I declined. He played the guitar again and sang, but I didn't listen.

The sunset wasn't spectacular. I wasn't paying attention anyway. Stephen was leaning back, his eyes half-closed. He said nothing. He just squinted out at San Francisco and the Marin headlands. I stared into the bay and observed a freighter make its way through the Golden Gate. The old black man noticed the freighter, too. I could see from the corner of my eye that he was leaning towards me. He stopped playing the guitar, leaned in close, and said, "You know, there's no way to get there now." I looked at him and frowned. Wind sighed in the shrubs behind us. He went on: "Everything is impossible without the threads of bridges! Socialism may be great for some folks but not for us. Imagine having an army march across that bridge. It'd fall down! Then you wouldn't be able to get back here. See what I mean?" He shrugged his shoulders, then slapped his thigh, then laughed. When he had calmed down he smiled triumphantly, as though he had delivered himself of precious wisdom. I shrugged *my* shoulders. He finished: "What do you see? See Alcatraz? See the Pyramid? See Treasure Island?" And then he started singing again.

Stephen tapped his temple at me. I nodded. I asked Stephen if we should go. The black man stopped playing the guitar and started swigging bourbon from the bottle. We stood to go, and the old man said good-bye, laughing to himself about something that we did not see or understand or care about. We nodded to him and the others, but as before, nobody acknowledged us. We went back to the car and drove down the hills towards Clem's place.

The next few weeks were crazy. What I wanted to do first was to find a job, anything, but the first few days I made little progress. I sat around the studio and watered the plants, rubbed mayonnaise into their leaves. The studio had a certain character about it, as if it had been a sixties crash pad and had never quite recovered. The paint was peeling, in quite large strips in some places. There was still a vague graffito on the ceiling, a large purple flower fading into the ceiling like a disappearing fresco in some Italian village church. The room was small and quite shabby. The bathroom was filthy, and the kitchen was crawling with a steady stream of cockroaches, which, in the middle of the night, rained down from the ceiling if the light was switched on.

The only windows in the room—on the north wall—overlooked a patio covered with a trellis interlaced with vines. Pizza and beer were served in the patio, and all day long—and all night long—a loudspeaker announced that customers' pizzas were ready. I would sit sometimes for hours staring down into the patio, just watching the people eat and drink. I sat and thought. I found I had come to a border, a very real frontier: the overwhelming reality that I had decided to reconstruct my life. It was a reality that stimulated me in the mornings and took me from office building to office building seeking employment, but that, by afternoon, left me bereft and depressed. I would return to the studio and stare out the window. I would think of everything that was finished—childhood, school, college. I would wonder what the next stage of my life would bring—for life is a proposition of many stages, of levels to which we rise or fall. Just as we are taught in grade-school history (Columbus discovered America in 1492; Rome fell in 476), our lives take dips and curves and sometimes magical leaps of fancy through raw air. To grasp the blue-burnished atmosphere of Berkeley and the bay, to renew myself in the contemplation of tangled vines, to learn the meanings of crowds, of noise and terror of dark streets—in short, to make a new life, again alone—this was the sudden agenda, and I trembled, one night, at the prospect. The familiar places and haunts were far off, unavailable. The people I had known were a hundred miles away, though at night they returned as ghosts in my dreams. They returned by day as well, in the faces of strangers I mistook for old friends. Walking along I would spot someone whom I surely knew. I would open my mouth and widen my eyes and then remember I was no longer home. That group there on the corner—I didn't know them after all. That man in the market—he wasn't Kevin or Fred. That young woman tossing her head just so—it wasn't Lisa.

So I would sit by the window and stare. I put the phone beside me, but it was silent. I knew no one, and during my daily treks about town, I met no one. One day, having found no work though I'd searched all day, I rested, watching the news, glancing out the window. As the afternoon lengthened I was filled with a deep sense of purposelessness again, as if nothing were waiting to be done, nobody waiting to call, and I remembered, with a clarity as sharp as a chill, those long and interminable days of my teenage years, when, after school had let out, I would struggle with two or three other kids to produce the high-school paper; and then, at home, before my stepfather came in to fix dinner with my mother—who would be the last to return from her office—I would lie aimless and lazy on the couch in the living room, regarding the news from Sacramento and San Francisco as though it were a communication from another planet. One entire living room wall had been of glass looking onto the river. I would sit alone and bored in that room as I stared at the river, its slow pace a metaphor for my life in that town, and as the afternoon lingered, as twilight began to close around the edges and claim reality, converting it to the fantasy world of silhouettes and shadows, I'd divide my attention alternately between the river and the news, as lonely and hopeful as any teenager can be.

I tried at that time—in those first few weeks in

Berkeley—to reach Ann in Oakland. Countless calls went unanswered, the phone ringing and tolling, the line never engaging. Finally, one afternoon, she answered.

"Where have you been?" I asked. "I've been here for weeks and I've tried to reach you the whole time."

"You're here!" she shrieked. "I should have told you . . . God, I didn't have a number for you, though . . . I had a chance to go to Massachusetts to stay at my aunt's place for a while. I just got back." Her voice was clear and, to my lonely ears, exceptionally sweet. "Let's get together right away," she said, "like tonight, okay?"

I agreed, and we met later in north Oakland, in a busy cafe lit entirely by candlelight. There were too many people there. The noise of conversation created a terrible din, and we had to shout at each other. She yelled her past few weeks to me, told me about the place in Massachusetts, a huge old mansion inhabited only by her widowed aunt. "The place seemed truly haunted," she shouted with a glint in her eye. "Anyway, I'm going back to stay for a bit. My aunt is lonely, and I offered to keep her company through the winter."

I nodded when she told me. I had hoped that now I was in the area, we could resume our friendship. I shouted to her about Clem's apartment, about how tough I was finding it to get a job. She agreed that it was impossible, but advised not to worry about it, " . . . and then, of course, something will just fall in your lap."

We ate pecan pie and drank espresso, so bitter and so strong that I began to shake with nerves. We sat for a long time and watched the other patrons, falling into an old game we used to play that analyzed an individual based simply on attire, expression, carriage, and tone of voice, if we could overhear them. "There, that one!" she pointed at a thirty-ish woman with page-boy hair. "She is so together, see the way she flings her head around? She *wants* to be an analyst, but she doesn't have the education. So she wants to be a writer, but she doesn't have any talent—which she doesn't know yet. She gets angry when confronted with someone who has accomplished something, maybe someone she knows has a friend who has published a book of poetry or short stories, and she gets truly upset about it. She goes home and tells herself: 'I have a study, I have a typewriter and a pencil, I drink lots of strong coffee and stare at the bay, so how come I can't write?' And then she paces in the throes of angst and finally ends the day here with her friends, as bourgeois and boring as you can get."

"Bravo!" I congratulated Ann on this complete, though fictional, biography. "How about him, over there?" I pointed, my finger aimed at a very pretty young man, his blond hair falling in a glistening sheet across one eye, his long, elegant neck barely holding his head. "He must trip and fall quite often," I said, "since his nose is so high in the air. He wants to *do something*, anything really, but he tends towards fashion design, or, he thinks, maybe modeling. But nothing happens, because he is truly quite lazy and just too young. His looks—that particular brand of blond pretty-boy—have branded him hopelessly effete. Ennui is his metier, his grounding, what little there is of it. He is often annoyed to be so instantly assumed to be queer, because although he does indeed consider himself gay, he feels he doesn't *act* gay. After all, he's just himself, isn't he? But what he really doesn't know *is* himself, but he doesn't know that yet."

"Good," Ann said, "though a bit convoluted at the end."

"Thank you." I inclined my head in mock deference.

"You know," Ann said over another cup of espresso, to which she added a great deal of cream and sugar, "I don't think you belong here, not in the East Bay."

I raised my eyebrows and sipped some water.

She went on, "San Francisco is the place for you. Why waste your time over here?"

I struggled to answer her question, which I took literally, though later I realized it had been simply rhetorical. "Because Stephen's here, and I have a place to stay."

She nodded. "Yes, because Stephen's here. How is he, anyway?"

"He's going to get married," I said.

She nodded again. "And do you see much of him and his girlfriend?"

I shook my head.

Ann was quiet for just a moment. "Do you have any money?"

I shook my head again. "No, I have about four hundred dollars left."

"I thought so," she said. "Look, I'm going back to Massachusetts next week, but before I go, I want to help you out, okay? Now don't go protesting or complaining or giving me any excuses, because I'm going to do it, and you're going to let me, and that's that."

She stopped and looked at me, sincerely, and a bit sternly, I thought. I shrugged my shoulders, and she went on, "Okay, then, I'll give you some money, which is yours to use until you get settled, and just so it won't be messy, you can pay me back when things are going all right for you later on."

It was a question, so I nodded and said, "Thank you."

She smiled, and so did I. In the absence of any clear plan of my own, hers seemed perfectly acceptable. Surely I couldn't lounge around Clem's studio forever, just staring out the window and wondering if and when I would actually begin to live my life. Hadn't I already had my share of false starts?

"Okay, then, get your stuff together, and I'll help you move to the city. It's no big deal, as far as distance goes, but the whole thing is really a different kind of place. I think it's what you're looking for."

And so I agreed—in what might have seemed a capitulation to her will, but was, really, a response to my own curiosity. Ever since my teenage years—waiting—San Francisco had shimmered in the back of my mind. I'd felt it like a secret waiting to be told. That I could so easily just pack up and go—with Ann's help—was mysterious to me in its simplicity (why had I not already done it, years ago?) and in its richness of promise.

One night, just before making the move across the bay, on a warm, temperate evening in late autumn, I sat one last time to stare at the patio below the studio. Someone had brought a guitar and sat playing amidst the people scattered there. The guitar, the singing, the soft humming all mixed and drifted to my window, but I was cold and restless. I had begun already to crave the pounding beat of dance music, the stares of dark, seeking eyes, and the love I knew they would promise. I remembered Keith's tales of the city, of the dance pavilions and clubs, of all the places I had yet to visit—and of which I had been afraid, so afraid that even while in Berkeley, I had failed to cross that bay and seek the promise of love and passion that I knew lay waiting. I got up and shut the window, drew the blinds, and went to bed.

I left after that, early the next morning. Ann drove me in my car. We rode in silence on that gloomy morning, until finally, looking over at the city, we saw the clouds part in a perfect halo around the white skyline of San Francisco. Ann shook her head and said, "It's magnificent, like an alabaster city." I glanced at the shine of the mist moving around the tall buildings and hills, but I said nothing. I didn't see alabaster, nor magnificence.

Later that evening, after I had settled into my new place—which Ann had found with ease for me the day before—I tried to call Stephen—I don't know why—but he wasn't there, and when I asked the woman who answered the phone when he would be back, she said she didn't know where he had gone or when he would be back, and then she abruptly hung up.

4

With its crystalline shine of sea-ripened air and vaporous waves of fog, San Francisco seemed completely unreal, most certainly misplaced, as though there should be nothing on the hills but windswept grasses—the rest done with mirrors. Later I learned the city rested on sand dunes and rock, as unpredictable and shaky as light reflected on water. Hills and valleys and great outcroppings of rock undulated beneath Mediterranean clumps of apartment buildings, Victorian houses, and elegant skyscrapers suspended by invisible forces above silt and sand glazed by concrete.

My first impression of the city was of its coldness, for in the midst of Indian summer great masses of fog moved over the city, thoroughly creating the dead of February though calendars declared that it was October. I shuddered in damp silence those first nights and looked at the city as one looks at a potential lover—shivering, anticipating, alert. The change from Berkeley was sudden and dramatic. Everything was different—the cold, the wind, the light, the unremitting ocean breeze. I remained vigilant, on guard at every sound, every shadow. Something moved at all times. There was never a moment of rest or deep silence, for the air and trees were in constant motion, as though spirits were forever passing through.

There were many ways to investigate the city those first days, and penetration of its men was among them. From the window of the tiny apartment Ann had arranged for me, I could see Buena Vista Park, a green lump up ahead, and I walked there often, in a ritual well practiced during those slow, hot nights in the country. Through the province of the bush queens threaded suggestions of paths, which, when followed, yielded blond boys and bearded men. Cold ocean breezes stirred the eucalyptus and pines as ceaselessly as the men beneath their branches moved.

But I found nothing of interest there, nothing to draw me back as I had been drawn to the grove in the college town. The silent eye-work was tedious and tried my patience, for I suspected that somewhere in the crowded city it was easier than that.

Sections of San Francisco were so distinctly different from others that the city seemed at odds with itself, schizophrenic perhaps. It was composed of too many communities, each so distinct and so contained that, though they might overlap, they never intersected. Chinatown and North Beach and the financial district rubbed shoulders, yet they didn't connect. I discovered the Mission District—comfortable to me in its sunny flatness—and Ocean Beach, frightening and haunted. It was all a great jigsaw, loosely fitted.

The beaches at Land's End or beneath the Cliff House lured me in those early weeks, though as I walked along them and heard the great combers thunder and the wind howl, I was edgy, expecting something horrible to spring from the cliffs or rise from the waves. The newspaper printed articles about a mysterious "emerald city," a mirage shimmering above the ocean off Point Reyes, and I remember that, years later, a friend fell into the habit of calling San Francisco the Land of Oz and telling of a haunted house at Stinson Beach and of ghosts wandering Mount Tamalpais in the windswept darkness.

But something addicted me to the beaches and to the craggy cliffs above. I wandered for hours along high trails or among pines and cypresses twisted into windy contortions until finally, one day, knowing every path and contour, the spell was broken.

The entire town was bewitching after that. Distances seemed too great, and my eye was forever tricked by shifting light and clouds. This *trompe-l'oeil* city befitted the setting of a medieval fairy tale, so intricate were its tribes and rituals. When I wanted to touch something concrete, I would go to the waterfront beneath the Bay Bridge and stand at the railing. But Treasure Island always led my eye to Angel Island, and I would crane my neck to find Alcatraz, out of sight. I would leave the glaring water and sit for hours by a concrete fountain downtown, where pedestrians could pass in and out of the fountain—its intricate waterfalls and angles concealed passageways that were perfectly dry. I would sit and study the walkers and the pigeons. I would stare at the sky and then up Market Street. I would think, remember, and try to understand what it was that made me feel so bereft.

It was the spirit of the town I felt, the magnetic fields or psychic waves—something beyond the human level. It was the incandescent light, shimmering like polished glass, the glare of aquamarine seas, surging and cold. It was a feeling that geography was displaced, that the scale of things was based on some exceptional formula. Rare visions presented themselves at unexpected moments: a half-moon veiled in luminescent mist; immense bridges shrouded in haze. I expected apparitions to materialize at any moment, specters to undulate in the half-light of a late summer's foggy dusk.

A friend once suggested that San Francisco was a city of wizards, that every resident was imbued with extraordinary magical powers, and in those first days I believed it. Glamor and celebrity were at hand: limousines sped past me in the windswept streets; elegant women strode arm in arm downtown, their fur collars raised high around their thin, wrinkled necks; cigarettes dangled from the lips of questionable young men who leaned in doorways against the bitter wind.

It was engagingly urban. I found myself in strangers' beds when I awoke, and I was filled with a sense of purpose, as though all my life I had awaited the opportunity to be anonymous. I began to explore the nightlife and the baths. My suspicion at the park was proven at the baths: There *was* an easier way to find evanescent passion. It was a kind of love that was easy and comfortable, that blossomed and faded even as one watched, a completely romantic ritual that left no residue of entanglement, just a lingering tickle for more, or perhaps for something else, something different.

Those evenings left no trace of loss or failure; there was no evidence that love had been and gone, unless love left its mark, undeniably discovered sometime later at the clinic. But hours and hours were passed in nothing but a tight white towel, waiting, searching, hoping.

I did everything. Early on a Saturday evening I would go to the bars to cruise and frustrate myself into the frenzy that, with the help of marijuana and Quaaludes, would give way to dancing, finally unleashing itself in hazy, blissful nights in the arms and on the backs of strangers, warm and damp, hungry and handsome. Saturday nights became Sunday mornings, all a blur of tanned male flesh, muscles tightening beneath the slightest caress, towels draping oddly over half-aroused men.

One night that fall I stood in a hedonistic trance against a wall at a huge warehouse-baths south of Market Street. I looked to my left and my eyes inspected a man whose face I knew but whose body I did not. A long, thoughtful stare gave way to memory: the face was Keith's, whose number I had kept in a drawer in the bureau for so long in that other town.

"But how did you do *that*?" I asked him that night as I nodded wide-eyed at his chest, shoulders, and arms.

He shrugged. "I call it 'the transformation' . . . that's what everyone does when they come to San Francisco."

I raised my eyebrows.

"Why are you here?" he asked.

I gave him the three-year wrap-up and inquired of his recent history.

"Well, I left that town right after I met you," he explained, "because I just couldn't take it anymore. I mean, the hiking boots and down jackets! And no one ever studied anyway. So I moved down here and undertook the beginning of the transformation, which took just exactly eleven months—the gym *every* day after work, some steroid shots, a ton of vitamins and tuna, running, and dancing my ass off at Trocadero every weekend. It's the only way to do it."

I nodded and was silent for a moment. I didn't know what to say next, but I was happy to have met a friend. I leaned against the wall and watched a blond boy sashay down the hall. The sound system blared a string of old hits. The Village People sang "Macho Man," and I laughed and said to Keith, "Your song now with all those muscles!"

He listened, then laughed. "You've got to come over real soon," he said. "Come downstairs and let me give you my card."

We went down to the lockers, and I noticed how very muscular he had become; it showed even more in motion. His neck was short and thick, his back a platter of ridges and knots. He walked differently because of it, a deep, affected macho swagger.

He reached into his locker and produced a grey business card that had printed on it only his name and phone number.

The next weekend he took me on a "tour" of the city, *his* tour through the baths and sex clubs he insisted were *de rigeur* with his crowd, which I gathered from the many nods and hellos was *the* crowd of muscle studs, all of whom exercised at the same gym and frequented the same bars and sex clubs.

It was late fall, and the weather had become quite unpredictable. Great storms moved across the city, coming always with the forewarning of brooding skies, which passed, then yielded to days so warm and so clear that one believed it was mid-June. That weekend of Keith's tour began with a thunderstorm on Friday night—lightning like neon illuminating the heavy skies. But, by early Saturday morning, a heat wave had settled, extracting energy and languishing the town. Later that weekend Keith would remark: "Can you imagine what this city would be like if we had regular summer weather? It would be absolutely wanton . . . sweat everywhere . . . I think the cold is like a mother here, keeping things in line."

That Saturday night he led me through bathhouses and sex clubs teeming with sexuality so constant and surging it was liquid, enfolding us in waves of lust and passion strobed red and orange by dim spotlights turned away from open space and aimed duplicitly into glass and mirrors. We toured dozens of monuments to male pleasure, Keith laying out a sizable fortune in entrance fees. We walked miles through warm, dark halls lined with warm, damp men, their impatience compounded by the unrelenting heat. I heard someone whisper, "Where *is* the fog?"

At one point that night I stopped short, pulled Keith close beside me for security, and took a deep breath. "I never imagined . . ." I started to say, but he only smiled.

"Yes, I suppose," he mused. "But really, it's nothing like it used to be, even all this . . ." He waved his arm about. "Even all this is not what it used to be. Just a couple of years ago, I guess about the time Dreamland opened and closed, there was more . . . how do I say it? . . . *je ne sais quoi* . . . more of a *joie de vivre*."

I made a face at him. "Stop it," I said.

"Oh such a queen!" he declared in his deepest macho voice. "What I meant to say was that it was more fun than this when it was all so new. But that was before the fall of the gay community."

"The what?" I said.

"Look," he said. "They shot Harvey Milk, okay?"

I nodded and kept my silence. All around me were male creatures of shocking beauty, of such perfection that one's only reasonable response was hyperventilation. They passed and crossed before, beside, and behind me, brushed their shoulders across my back: fleshy gossamer. I swore I felt electricity in the air. For a moment I feared the heat wave had set up an unnatural conduction between my body and all those perfect animals around me—I was afraid of lightning. And then I looked at Keith and thought of the transformation. I looked down at my own body, so fine my whole life, but that night I became self-conscious in my white towel; my body was only good.

Keith saw me glance at my chest. "You'll have to join the gym."

I shrugged my shoulders.

He went on: "Look, if you want to be one hundred percent masculine so you can get dates, you've got to join the gym and become a hunk." But his remark was cut short by distraction, my distraction. A remarkable man led my eye, and then my body, away from Keith, and for an hour I felt as if I were discovering something new. Later I found Keith waiting impatiently in the lounge, and he insisted I crash at his place.

His apartment was a tiny, precise one-bedroom affair with a view, the converted attic of a Victorian in Dolores Heights. The view was so spectacular that one felt exclamations were required, lest the skyline might up and vanish in indignation. Pretensions of taste were everywhere: two exquisite Navajo rugs; dusty crystal displayed on an antique buffet; slick museum posters framed in flat black metal; and a beveled mirror that reflected the bed. I took a blanket and pillow and curled up in the couch and went to sleep, as content as a man who has just come home from a long trip and found everything in order, even the garden has blossomed.

The next morning Keith made breakfast, and the rest of that weekend was spent in hearing Keith's biography, quite passionately confessed as though I were the Bishop of San Francisco. Keith originally came from Sedalia, Missouri, but his folks had moved the family to Barstow when he was ten. Desert life predominated his coming to awareness, and its evidence—he indicated the Navajo rugs and a tiny cactus on the bookshelf—betrayed his inner feelings as well. Life seemed to him a rather vast, open place, in which one had to work hard and examine oneself and others carefully to find details that mattered, the cut of a beard, the tone of a voice. His college life, in that country town where we first met so briefly, had been the point of his coming out, which was to him an act of salvation. And so San Francisco had become his only possible home, a point of view I would come to share.

Later Keith took me to his gym, and I exercised with him, discovering to my dismay that the population of the gymnasium comprised a separate tribe of deliriously beautiful men. Their beauty did not fill me with desire, as I might have expected, nor lust, but I found instead a strong urge to become one of them, to perform the daily rituals that would, at some future point, confer upon me the status of beauty that these creatures enjoyed.

And so I began—and how I loved it. Surrounded by others who mirrored the same motions, I was elevated not only by the catharsis of muscular strain, but also by the mutuality of common purpose, which revealed the deeper meaning of the experience—to build a body that would be worthy of love.

The common purpose of the gym enfolded and emboldened me. Friends were made by happenstance introduction, through Keith, or through accident of shared equipment. A dreamworld that I had glimpsed only through shades of envy, desire, and hope opened itself to me and beckoned me to come along. I met Keith's immediate circle of friends—Cap, the blond muscleman who drove a limousine for a living; Laine, the sexy, silent banker whose ruling passions in life were said to be teddy bears and motorcycles; and The Witch, who, Keith explained, was really named Peter, but whose reputation and attitude had earned him the title The Witch, " . . . but don't ever let him know we call him that."

November passed into December as we exercised and sought sex, a plain life that seemed always precursory to something, though we never knew what. We suspected that something big was about to happen. One might find a lover tomorrow or next week. Fame would somehow find us and enrich life immeasurably. A distant rich relative would die and unbeknownst to us leave a sizable fortune (rumor had it that one member of the gym had inherited—suddenly and to his surprise—six million dollars, all in one day). We always expected something amazing, something that would change our lives forever.

We lived on the fringes of the glamorous life, patiently vigilant, working hard to achieve physical perfection. It was all new and exciting, filling me with energy every morning when I awoke, and my memories began to fade as if I were suddenly recuperating from a lengthy illness, those distant memories of college, of Stephen, of Alison, of Ann gone to Massachusetts. Habits—of the gym, of late afternoon strolls, of Saturday nights at the baths—were immediately adopted as I began to run with that crowd, and from these new habits I received a sense of security, of belonging, at long last.

The city approached winter the way an old woman crosses the street—reluctantly but necessarily, making slow fits and starts, until finally, one morning in late December, I awoke to find the apartment exceedingly chilly in the silver light of winter dawn. The fog had vanished with October and November, and as a subtle mood of winter fell over the city, there were increasingly more days of bright, clear sunshine, through which blew the constant cold wind, never ceasing, that wind which, in winter, was less ghostly but more insulting, each cold blast a stinging slap.

It was several weeks before I understood how constant the bitter cold and sweeping winds were in the city, how utterly *normal* they were. That winter I often compared San Francisco to Chicago, suggesting that surely San Francisco was the windier city—until one day an endearing middle-aged woman who worked in the offices of the business I had joined as a clerk disabused me of my belief that the reference to Chicago as the "windy city" was related to weather. She explained that the phrase referred to the ferocious politicians of Chicago who created so much "wind."

Then I came to love the wind, embracing it as if it were some unique feature devised exclusively for my enjoyment of San Francisco, for I had, in all those years growing up in the parched and motionless air of the interior, fantasized often of violent storms and brooding skies. I had longed for the gothic: cold castles, dank dungeons, thunder, lightning. I fell into the habit of walking long into late afternoons and evenings, walking into the wind, anywhere. It seemed as though the wind actually swept the streets, so deserted were they on winter evenings. The steep angles of hills, the brisk wind, the general harshness of the city drove people indoors at that time of day, at that time of year, and I was free to stroll alone, like an evil despot inspecting his purview, the frightened denizens trembling and silent behind drawn curtains and closed doors.

One day in early January I ran into Keith's friend Cap, whom I hadn't seen at the gym for several weeks. "I've been busy with Christmas," he shrugged. "Why don't you come up for some coffee?" He pointed to his house just up the street. We drank coffee and looked out the windows as twilight fell, and we played cards. Three times he held the winning hand, so I stopped playing and asked him to tell me about himself.

"There's not much to tell," he began. He rose and struck a match into the fireplace. A blaze crackled, illuminating the room with orange shadows. He lit a cigarette and settled his heavy body into the couch beside me. "I grew up on an island off the coast near Atlantic City. Once a week we took the boat ashore to do the shopping. There was a one-room schoolhouse, and this was in the fifties!" He drew on his cigarette and stared out the window. "I was married a long, long time ago. I was very much in love with her, but she just asked me to leave one day, and that was that. Afterward, I realized that what I had always considered passing fancy—you know, occasionally *allowing* a young guy to suck me off in the subway station, or maybe fucking a boy prostitute when I was in New York—well, I realized I was a fag. That I was gay. So I moved to San Francisco, and I've been here for ten years now—"

I interrupted, "But you were in school in the fifties?"

"I'm thirty-eight now," he said. "I came to San Francisco when I was twenty-eight. I was married when I was twenty."

I nodded. Outside, twilight had given way to night, but the black sky was filled with clouds moving in, blowing fast over the city, illuminated yellow by the halogen lamps of Market Street. Cap got up and put a tape on the stereo, turned it down low. "I've really loved San Francisco," he went on. "There's nothing like it. You know, when I first got here, there was none of this." He gestured towards the window, towards the Castro neighborhood below. "We built it all from nothing, in just a few years. When I first came, I worked a day job and a night job, saved enough money to buy this house. Then I started to buy others, fix them up, and sell them at an enormous profit. Whenever you read about the way the Castro was transformed during the seventies, about how gays bought the old Victorians and renovated them and resold them to other gays, well, I was one of the ones who did that."

"What do you do now?" I asked, and then remembered he was a chauffeur.

"Not much" he answered. "I stopped renovating houses. I'd made enough money in five years to last the rest of my life. So I drive a limousine four nights a week. It can be very, very interesting. I've chauffeured everyone from Katharine Hepburn to Hugh Hefner to Angie Dickinson. Talk about a campy job!" He laughed, then became quiet, smoking and staring out the window at the thickening clouds. "What about you?" he asked. "You're Keith's friend, that's all I know."

I nodded. "I moved here last fall, from up north, where I went to college. My family is in the valley, up at the top near the foothills. I studied anthropology and history—absolutely useless—and now I'm here. I work downtown, part-time office work. That's all."

He nodded. Then the phone rang. "Excuse me," he said, and he went into another room to take the call. I looked out over the city and saw that it had begun to rain just then, very gently, though the wind blew the fine drops into a mesh, a shifting mist. Cap's tape was running. I stared out at the drizzle. Fritz Wunderlich sang "Die Rose von Stambul," then a portion from Tosca cut in, Maria Callas singing out her ferocious tensions. Suddenly, Barbra Streisand sang "I Believe in Love."

Cap returned. "Oh god, the Barbra Streisand tape!" he exclaimed. "My old boyfriend made this tape for me. I used to complain about Barbra Streisand, and he'd say I couldn't really be gay if I didn't like Barbra. Once he asked me, 'Doesn't every queer want to be Barbra Streisand when they grow up?' Well, I didn't like that very much, and I told him so, but he could never quite understand it."

"Who was he?" I asked.

"Oh, you know him from the gym—Peter. But everyone calls him The Witch."

"Do you know why?" I asked.

Cap shrugged his shoulders. "You know, on a trip to L.A. once, he and I stopped outside Grauman's Chinese Theater, and I can still remember how Peter nodded at the theater with all the reverence of a Roman Catholic gazing upon the Holy See of St. Peter's Basilica and said, 'That's where I first saw *Funny Lady.*'"

I shook my head. For two months now I had observed The Witch at the gym, and for two months he had neither spoken to me nor acknowledged that we had met. I assumed it was part of the bad manners I found everywhere in evidence in the city. Cap's story stirred my curiosity about The Witch, but I asked nothing more.

Finally, Cap said he had to go to bed, but he asked me to come over again anytime, suggested perhaps we could have dinner soon. I agreed and left, walking into that cold, misty rain, wondering what to do with the evening. It was Friday night, and I had no plans. I walked down Castro Street and stepped into a bar. It was nearly empty, though the music boomed as if accompanying a festival. I left and walked up to Market Street, turned, and began to walk down Market. I thought of nothing, but I kept my eyes alert; there had been too many reports of violence. All I wanted to do was walk.

I ended up south of Market, walking and looking, its streets and alleys dipping occasionally, the evidence of subterranean rivers draining into the bay. In some alleys I saw old buildings slanted at severe angles, looking like haunted houses. One such building tilted staggeringly forward and bore the telling sign of a business long since bankrupt and forgotten: Terra Incognita. I loved the area, its streets filled with sudden, unique visions: leathermen haunting the alleys by night, searching for demons and feigned glory; and clones who adorned themselves in nothing but skintight jeans and T-shirts in even the coldest weather, standing for hours beside rough wood railings overlooking rooms of leather and smoke. And there were the sex clubs and bathhouses, the sanctuaries of pleasure through which Keith had shown me the way, and through which I had come to know my main source of sexual satisfaction. This was the sexual life—to wander through those alleys, to pass hours in a sex club, to wait outside a bar at closing time in the hope that someone would make an advance, or even a gesture, to walk home in the cold and bleak silence before dawn with one's clothes wrinkled and stinking of tobacco, beer, and sweat, to enter one's apartment at four or five in the morning and shake one's head in disbelief at the waste of so many hours given to seeking sex, seeking companionship, only to arrive tired, cold, and forlorn with nothing but hope and fatigue to sustain the balance of the darkness until, given the sunrise and opening of a bright, clear, and painfully luminous day, one shrugged one's shoulders and reasoned that the sum total of man's existence amounted to nothing more than the comfort of improved housing, electric blankets, and the gluttonous opportunity to press onward with greater ease to the next orgasm.

That night I wandered the streets, those streets with names that taunted the imagination with ghostly evocations: Folsom, suggestive of the prison, of leather, of hardness; or Natoma, evoking images of an Indian maiden once gathering grasses in those now cemented marshes; or Isis Alley, summoning images of Egyptians flattened against a scroll, their hands and feet pointed like dancers at Trocadero; or Mission and Howard and Sixth and Fifth, which all by association with skid row were remindful of the depths to which one had yet to sink.

I spent an hour at the Eagle, speaking to no one. I observed the men until bored, then moved on to the Brig, which, crowded though it was, revealed nothing new, nothing tantalizing. So I walked a few yards to a sex club, entered, and leaned against the back wall. In the dim light I sat and waited to see, barely able to discern the chalk drawings on the wall: a young stud being sodomized by two burly musclemen. The club was deserted at that hour, for the bars had yet to close. The speakers threw disco music at the empty space like a raging child punching the air in frustrated anger. Occasionally the music stopped while the attendant in the booth up front changed the tape, and street sounds would filter through the front door: the roar of a motorcycle; the honk of an angry motorist's horn; the shrieking laughter of a group of leathermen passing by, their voices more shrill than those of the tired old queens of the skirt and sweater set.

I moved away from the wall, lit a cigarette that I did not smoke but held only against boredom, and walked around the club. My boots crunched against the concrete. Grace Jones sang "Warm Leatherette." I opened the door to a cubicle and let it shut just to hear the creaking of the hinges in the loneliness of so much empty space. I walked into the back room, as deserted as the rest of the club. I walked past video games and pinball machines, their unattended panels flashing and clicking into the empty darkness. Where was everyone? I asked myself; it was getting late.

In the rear, Grace Jones was vaguely audible from up front, distant and retreating as I moved. I could hear my breathing. I stepped to a small patio outside, let the creaky door slam shut behind me. It was very dark, and I stumbled. I clung to the wall and decided to go back inside, but for a moment I looked straight up at the night sky, a dull orange reflection of the city beneath. Wind rustled the leaves of a crisp, dying shrub beside me, and I noticed the mist had gone. I retreated into the club once again.

Men had begun to arrive, and I reckoned that it must have just passed two o'clock in the morning. With the bars closed, the door played a staccato of buzzes, as, one after another, men adorned in leather were admitted to the club. I strolled in endless circles between the rows of cubicles, each providing a tiny room for sex. Small windows set in each door allowed a glimpse of whoever waited inside. I walked around and around, stopping to bend and peer into each cubicle, examining the possibilities: young men wearing nothing but jockstraps reclined and raised their legs provocatively; old men sat trembling in anticipation of even a glance from a passing stranger; leathermen wearing serious expressions stood ready for worship.

I could not find a connection, could not feel the things I had hoped to feel. My lust was intact, for surely many of the men were attractive and beckoning, but I felt an edge of danger or puzzlement. Things weren't right. I was uncomfortable and tense. The mood of the place was eerie, as though something were about to happen. I felt dizzy, as if my heels were sinking into the floor, throwing me off balance. I clung to the wall for support. It was trembling. The building creaked and groaned. Fixtures swung as if moved by spirits and someone shouted: "Earthquake!"

The dim lights flickered, went off, came back on. I didn't move. Then I felt the floor roll, and the whole building shook violently. Men scrambled out of the booths, clutching their clothes and shoes close to their bodies or stuffing their shirttails frantically into their pants. They looked around indecisively and saw that everyone else was as unsure as they. I remained against the concrete wall now shaking like a leaf in an autumn wind, and then, suddenly, it stopped. Everyone looked around, unspeaking, uncertain what to do or where to go next, too wary to resume the cruise. I left hastily and welcomed the open street. Some people had emerged onto the streets and stood nervously laughing in small groups, but I ignored them and walked home.

5

That winter I devoted myself to the gym, content just to be amongst those men who seemed—when one spotted them on the street far removed from the setting of the gymnasium, say, lurking before a store window downtown, exclaiming to their friends over the cut of a Calvin Klein jacket or Perry Ellis trousers, or perhaps wandering aimlessly in North Beach, glancing at the bright sex palaces and their gaudy displays, or, late at night, walking alone up Market Street and looking every bit the picture of the starlet who has failed the screen test, or, sometimes, looking like the lost boy from Ohio whose dreams were not coming true and whose life, indeed, was going in no direction he would have ever foreseen, all the more tragic in a city redolent of newness and hope—those men seemed like ambassadors from this corner of male beauty to the general city at large, so exquisite were their faces, their physiques, and their fashions. Exercise was one way to achieve such status as a beauty missionary, and it bred a longing for fine clothes, tasteful surroundings, and luxurious transport. It was an obsession that had as its source a feeling that lay somewhere between hope and desperation. Daily we entered that glass-encased torture chamber, which reeked of soap and sweat, its front windows streaked with steam—which appeared at first glance to be sweat, until one realized that of course windows don't sweat, it was the steam of the heat of muscular men—and we squatted and bent and pushed and yanked against cables and iron until our bodies ached in every joint and every cell, and we amused ourselves with notions of *the pump*, which, after weeks and months and years, yielded the highly valued physical form that we worshiped as butch, as complete, as deserving of praise, fine clothes, serious sexual desire, and perhaps love.

We never spoke of such qualities as honesty, intelligence, courage, or warmth, for, as Keith and The Witch used to say, "Anything worth having may as well come wrapped in a nice package." The philosophy was simple: Upon achievement of physical beauty, one became entitled to receive love. As proof, we watched a particular young man that winter, a boyish blond newcomer who embarked upon a beauty regimen that shamed us all, his slender body swelling through December, January, and February, until one day in early spring we were forced, as our group strolled bare-chested down Castro Street, to acknowledge his exceptional, though newly developed, body—the body of a man, of a creature we would call "hunk" or, on Tuesdays or Wednesdays, when midweek doldrums fattened us in the mirrors, we might concede in utter desperation that the youngster had indeed elevated himself to the chiseled status of a god. That we felt *forced* to acknowledge his achievement betrayed our shallow cynicism and our despair, for he had, by way of his swollen pectorals and bulging triceps, done exactly what was believed could be done—he had snagged one of the city's most desirable faggots, the muscle-bound demigod of the gym circuit, a businessman whose holdings included a sizable downtown building, a string of health clubs, a Ferrari, a marble mansion at Sea Cliff, and a black Jeep.

There were other things in life as well, things to have and to see, places to visit, friends to make. Like the constant visions of striking beauty that confronted one at every turn, be they mountains or men, there were abiding things of value, value being determined by the ability to give pleasure: other perfect men; the Castro Theatre with its gaudy interior and trembling organ; rows of precise Edwardian homes and dignified Victorians; limousines that climbed the hills with ease and deposited their occupants at L'Etoile or Magnin's, Gump's or Saks; the flower-lined bedlam of Lombard Street, which, one block after straightening out, runs past the house to which a friend once pointed and shrieked, "The Vertigo house! Where Jimmy Stewart lived in *Vertigo!*"—which impressed me at the time and filled me with a schizophrenic sense of an unbridgeable gap between movies and real life, so fitting in a city whose vistas seemed like dreams; the pretentious beliefs of the natives that because of its crowds and grey iciness San Francisco was somehow allied with the East, to which San Franciscans constantly referred in the most familiar of terms, adopting always the word "Manhattan" over "New York," "*The*

East" over "Back East"—a supposed alliance that, to the natives, bestowed a courage to assume what they believed to be Eastern manners—haughtiness, bad driving, loud voices, and the poor taste to display one's worst emotions and personal crises on the street.

Through it all I moved in arrogant smugness, feeling as though I had *arrived*. Honking horns; streets inky with rain; rude, pressing throngs; and the daring freedom to yield to the allure of beautiful men—these elements instilled in me a precious mood of sophistication, a feeling that I had finally escaped the curse of rurality, of having been a lonely and unbelonging dreamer.

But friendship and acceptance were not as easily won as might have been expected. Though now we all belonged to a community, there was yet a strange anxiety among us, an insurmountable restraint I didn't understand. So much came to bear on so little the day I turned to The Witch in the gym and asked: "Why do you suppose some of these guys look so grouchy all the time?" To which he turned to me in utter astonishment and bristling approval and delivered himself of a soliloquy I would never forget: "My dear," he addressed himself to me in wavering low tones, "those precious young men are suffering from what is called 'perfect syndrome.' Have you watched them closely? Here and outside the gym? They spend their lives in pursuit of utter perfection. They work out at the gym every day, very hard, so their bodies are perfect. They spend unbelievable amounts of their hard-earned money—which they earn in a variety of interesting and incredibly ambitious careers to which they devote themselves with fascist gusto—on everything that will enhance their looks and preserve their youth: facials, tans, lotions, manicures, perfect haircuts, vitamins, meditation, bodywork, shiatsu, anabolic steroids, distilled water, natural foods, self-help books, workshops on how to build relationships, vacations, custom shoes, pillows, futons, and amino acids. They've worked very hard to buy the perfect car, which they keep in immaculate condition. Their apartments are absolutely taut, they're so painfully, tastefully clean and polished. Everything—*every little thing*—in their lives has been calculated, weighed, and chosen to such a degree that they're utterly miserable! They're exhausted! So of course they're grouchy! They're horribly lonely, but they think that if *they* can put that much work out to have everything so wonderful, then *you* better damn well have your shit together just as well. And if you *don't*. . . well!. . . you're not worth jack-shit. If I'm going to go to that much trouble, then so should you! Consequently, nobody measures up. So they keep scrubbing and polishing and acquiring one more piece of Baccarat crystal or one more state-of-the-art electronic piece of shit because . . . well, because everything's got to be in order, ready and waiting for that special, equally perfect man. Of course, their credit histories tell all."

I asked what he meant by this last remark. "Well, whenever I meet a potential boyfriend," he explained, "I run a credit check on him at the office. If he's got bad credit, forget it! I'm not going to judge someone based on the degree of his superficial perfection, no sir. The credit tells the story!"

And then he smiled at me and said, "I never thought you were *ever* going to say hello to me! But you remember, don't you? Keith introduced us a long time ago."

I told him of course I remembered, that's why I'd spoken. It was just that I was shy.

"Watch out then," The Witch said. "Shy and snob look the same way around here."

I nodded and appraised my visage in the wall mirrors—my countenance serious, my brow slightly furrowed, my lips sealed in a grimace that amazingly felt to me like a half-smile. I smiled openly and laughed.

"What's so funny?" The Witch asked as he leaned into a forward position and began to work his chest muscles with the cables.

"Nothing, just the way I looked when you said that," I answered. "I looked as grouchy as the rest of them."

The Witch nodded in a knowing way. "Exactly. It's tricky stuff," he grunted as he completed his set. "Gym etiquette is very delicate," he went on. "But stick around me for a while and you'll learn *everything* you need to know."

I smiled again and wondered at Peter's nickname, The Witch. No one had been more friendly. There wasn't a trace of venom or snobbery. His smile seemed genuine, and he was naturally handsome, though his body was unnaturally muscular, too much. His dark brown eyes darted everywhere when he spoke, as if alert to the possibility that something wonderful was about to happen and he didn't want to miss it. I noticed he wore a gym shirt that said, "This is not a dress rehearsal."

We went out to dinner that night to a tiny French restaurant near Potrero Hill. The room was filled with men leaning graciously across linen, china, and candles to whisper, confess, and dish the other patrons, their breath disturbing the candle flames, or rustling the centerpiece roses, falling finally in silence on warm bread steaming in straw baskets.

I learned that The Witch came from Miami by way of the gay circuit: New York, Houston, and Los Angeles. He had been in San Francisco for six and a half years, the first three of which had been spent "hustling and building up this impossible body!" He had been involved with Cap—"that beautiful blond hunk!"—but had recently taken an interest in a "young man from another gym."

"Who is he?" I asked.

"Oh, no one you'd have met yet," he answered. "But maybe he'll come to the gym with me next week if I can talk him into it. Probably not, though . . ."

"Is he your boyfriend?" I asked.

"Not quite yet. But I'm working on it."

We were silent as platters of steaming fish were set before us. I looked down at my plate and scrutinized the pink and white flakes that mingled with rice and herbs and a hot vegetable paste of yellow squash, pumpkin, spinach, and spices. Satisfied that there were no bones in the fish, I began to eat. The Witch closed his eyes and moaned as he tasted the fish. "Unbelievable!" he declared. "Absolutely wonderful!"

We ate in silence for a few minutes.

"You'll have to meet everyone," he said, putting his fork down and sipping his wine. "I'll see to it that you're introduced to the very best crowd at the gym."

"I think I've met quite a number already," I answered.

He raised his eyebrows. "Oh? Who?"

"Well, there's Keith, of course. And then Cap, your old boyfriend . . ."

He nodded.

"Then I met Laine, too, and a few others."

"Well, that's the core group, certainly" he said. "But you've yet to meet Tony and Drew and . . . well, the rest of the crowd."

"Tell me about Laine," I asked. "I know about you and Keith and Cap, but not about Laine."

He shrugged his shoulders. "Well, I don't know that there's so much to tell." His tone suggested the contrary. "Laine works downtown for a bank. He collects teddy bears, his apartment is full of them! And he's been going to the gym almost as long as I have, though with obviously less success . . . personally I don't find him especially attractive, at least not physically. Although you might."

It was a question, not a statement, and I shook my head. "No, not especially, though Keith thinks he's sexy, I think."

"Oh, I *know*," The Witch said. "It's all that hair. Keith adores men with hairy chests and backsides. He can hardly get it up unless his partner has a tush that looks like the floor of a barbershop! Me, I just don't see it. Laine's just too dark and too hairy and just too . . . too . . . standoffish, if you know what I mean . . ." His voice trailed off as his eyes followed a tall, beautiful man leaving the room. The Witch caught his eye and smiled, but the beauty shifted his gaze as if The Witch were invisible. "Well!" The Witch declared. "As if!"

I suppressed a smile. After a moment I asked, "Why?"

"What?"

"Why is Laine so shy?"

"I didn't say 'shy', I said 'standoffish'," he corrected me. Then he shrugged his shoulders. "Lord knows. I just don't know what anybody could see in him, but he's a part of the group, been around forever. Unlike you, new-comer." He fixed me with a stare. I took a long drink from my wine glass. I had the uneasy feeling he was intent on seduction, but I was disinclined.

The waiter brought more wine. The Witch poised his glass in midair and then, without sipping, set it down and said, "Well, like I said, any friend of Keith's is a friend of mine." I smiled but said nothing. He asked, "How do you know Keith?"

"College," I answered. "We tricked once in a park and then . . ."

"Oh dish!" he proclaimed, clapping his hands. "In a park?"

I nodded. "After that we didn't see each other until really very recently, here in the city, just after I moved. I hardly recognized him, but the connection goes back . . ."

"Wait until I tell Cap that you met Keith tricking in a park!"

"It was no big deal," I said.

He shrieked. "Even better! You're precious, you're precious! You've made my evening!"

I shrugged. "Really, it wasn't . . ."

"Oh, I know, I know, but dish is dish, dirt is dirt, haven't you ever seen *The Women*?"

I shook my head.

"No matter," he said. "It never hurts to have some little item of gossip tucked away, especially on someone as cocky and sanctimonious as Keith. But then, with a dick that size he can act any way he wants to, don't you agree?"

I shrugged my shoulders and sipped my wine.

"Oh, come on," The Witch said. "Keith's got substantial meat, a good body, *and* a good-paying job and a nice apartment. Everything!"

I sat demurely as he proceeded to deliver himself of the demographics of the gym: " . . . and so Tom has attitude because he's got ten inches! . . . and that Cuban guy with the tits and the Mercedes? Over eleven! Uncut! And thick! . . . and the hunky 'straight' guy? She's got a huge piece, absolutely enormous . . . no meat on the little blond dancer, though, so don't bother, you practically have to send out a search party . . . and then there's Cap! Oh Cap . . . such a big boy—"

I cut in, "And what about you?"

"Well!" He looked astonished for only a moment before saying, "Touché, darling. You'll fit right in."

The conversation stopped. My stomach tightened as if I were about to be sick on the table. The lights dimmed. The music softened, and I saw myself reflected in a gilded mirror across the room: distorted by marble appliqué. Lonely and victimized, that's how I suddenly felt, as though the chandeliers and silver were simply deigning to serve me—other, more esteemed patrons were yet to arrive. I looked at The Witch as though desperate for attention.

He didn't see me. He was contemplating his wine glass, as if it were a crystal ball. I took a deep breath and looked away. I hid my face in a long drink of water. The lights were brighter, the music gayer.

"Where do you live?" asked The Witch as coffee was served. I sighed in relief, a new topic.

"I have a tiny studio on Haight Street, just up from Divisadero. I can see Buena Vista Park out my window."

"That's handy," he said, but I only shrugged. The waiter brought cream. For a moment The Witch hummed something, and then stopped. I recognized the tune.

I said, "'More Than You Know'?"

"Wonderful!" he exclaimed. "I just *adore* Barbra Streisand so much. Oh, you're going to fit *right* in. We'll be the *best* of friends. Do you have a boyfriend?"

I analyzed his tone: gossip-mongering. "No," I answered.

"Oh well, then, who was your *last* boyfriend?"

"I've never had a boyfriend," I said.

"What?" he said. "Never been in love? Oh, my you *are* a neophyte, aren't you?"

I nodded and shrugged. "I'm not quite a virgin."

"No, of course not," he said. "But no boyfriends!"

The waiter suddenly hovered, and I looked up at him like a sinner at the foot of the cross. He blessed us with the check, which he applied to the table between us before withdrawing in silence like a phantom intruder. I felt suddenly curious about something, as if lost, the way one feels upon waking in the middle of the night, unable to remember the city or the date, or even to recognize the room. The evening was over, and I excused myself and left the restaurant, wandering through that dim district, drifting towards my neighborhood across town.

Many times that winter I felt that way—confused but curious, not remembering where I was, and uncertain about the next step. I would turn, in evening, away from the rich haze of sundown and look east to the rising moon, luminous like a pale girl, hurting. In the night I would awake and stare at my room until recent memory forced recognition: my apartment; San Francisco; my decisions. Something often nagged at the back of my mind, as if calling out for a firm decision, a course of action, though I never knew anything other than this imprecise mood. Somewhere, moving amongst us all, was a mood of disquiet, of something terribly amiss—though this feeling surfaced only occasionally, on those infrequent nights when we lay in bed unable to sleep, looking up into the darkness and trying to remember just what it was that we were hoping for.

It was a season of transition, though at the time we moved through it all in utter oblivion. There was too much rain that year, but we never noticed. We existed for the gym (for what it could make of us) and for each other. We became workout partners—Cap and The Witch and I—and we forced ourselves to try harder, to lift heavier weights. We gossiped and rocked with laughter between sets as we dished the unfavored members of the club. "I don't care what they look like," said both Cap and The Witch repeatedly. "But it's that bad attitude!"

"Everybody in the city has bad manners, though," I ventured one evening. "I noticed it the first day I moved here, and it just seems to get worse."

It was my turn to do the bench press, so I lay back and grunted while The Witch said, "There's a world of difference between bad manners and attitude."

"That's right," Cap agreed, not elaborating.

I finished my set and got up. "Go on," I said. "What's the difference?"

Cap lay down and started to pump the weight. The

Witch turned to me and pointed across the gym at a pair of young men, each blond, each appearing as young as teenagers, though they were probably in their twenties. "*That* is bad manners," he said, and just as he spoke, one of the young men snarled at an older man who had merely excused himself to pass by. The Witch scanned the gym, his eyes searching until he found another victim, to whom he pointed and said, "And *that* is attitude!" A dark-haired man with huge muscles and a heavy dark moustache sat up proudly, drummed his hands on the bench, and turned his head imperiously to gaze with disdain out the window.

"I knew the difference," I said as I lay back to do another set.

Such exchanges were common among us. Keith and I would exercise together, or Cap and I, or The Witch and I—or many other combinations—and throughout it all we analyzed, dissected, criticized, discovered, loved, and hated the whole thing—the gym, life in the Castro, in San Francisco, in general.

Our circle closed to include only the core group, but Laine remained always a mystery man, to whom Cap, Keith, and The Witch would cross the floor to greet and chat for a few moments, but with whom we never exercised. I suspected there was someone among us he didn't favor—or with whom there had been bad blood, so I kept my distance.

That was a time like a precipice, upon which we all crowded, pushing, as if wondering just who might be the first to jump. The season was cold, and right before Valentine's Day it got colder, so cold that I stayed in one weekend, wrapped myself in a blanket and stared at the television. I made tea and sat in the middle of the floor in silence. I put Brahms on the stereo and slept. I thought about the stories I heard at the gym. I wondered if I would relax.

The mood passed by the middle of the next week, but beneath it all lingered that sense of impatience and curiosity like a thread unraveling from a new sweater that cost too much: there was dissatisfaction. I slept badly in February, nights filled with phantoms and Valium. Mornings were slow, and memories afflicted afternoons, memories gilded by fiction. I dreamed all day and lay restless at night. I would lie on my stomach with my fists beneath my chest and fear that my heart would stop beating. Some nights I sat up and watched late movies and remembered my sister's years spent closed away in her room, the TV blaring. Other nights I proclaimed myself utterly insane and yielded to the miracles of pharmacy, likening myself to Neely O'Hara and passing into cloudy dreams of other times, of voices echoing in cathedrals, strange lights in the night sky. Once, late in February that winter, I couldn't sleep all night, and I sat by my window and listened: distant sirens; a dog barking; the rise and fall of laughter passing in the darkness. It was my habit those long, sleepless winter nights, to lie in the dark safely in bed and stare at the ceiling above, without color or shape, tears running down my cheeks. It seemed to be nothing in particular, just life. Disquiet ruled those nights. Impatience infected the days. Sometimes, passing in or out of sleep, a great peace settled over me, a peace as heavy and satisfying as the thick wool blanket under which I rested. But the source of that peace eluded me, vanishing the instant I struggled to secure it. I knew I wanted that tranquillity forever, but time moved on, and one moment faded to the next. It was inevitable, universal law—silence to nerves to stillness and despair.

By the Ides of March it had rained steadily for six weeks. My apartment began to smell damp. A cold wind never ceased howling through the pipes in the well that opened off the bathroom window. Rain tore homes from the hillsides, and I had to replace three umbrellas.

In April the rain stopped, but winter did not give up. Harsh winds swept the streets and kept us indoors— more time to think, to wait, and to make the high point of the day the gym, with its warmth, its men, its physical euphoria.

That winter I began to understand how Peter had earned his title The Witch. For while he was charming and kind enough to those of us among that tiny inner circle, he regarded others with contempt. And even among the accepted, desirable crowd, Peter could become vicious and snapping if an offense, real or imagined—and there were many—was made. Peter was a contradictory, contrary fellow. While disdaining others for attitude and poor manners, he exhibited the haughtiest condescension. His own beauty was held up at all times for admiration—the way a priest elevates the monstrance for worship—and any failure to remark on the size of his chest or the gleam in his eye (whenever it was intimated he needed such praise) led to swift denunciation. He even admitted one day, in joking, that he came to the gym not to hone his physique but to sharpen his tongue. He

passed judgment on others with ease and amazing rapid-
ity—"too much attitude," or "terrible, terrible credit," or
"an awful, tired thing . . . look at those love handles!" Yet
those of us who befriended The Witch remained
friendly for precisely the reason we should have abandoned him: we were afraid to become objects of his
scorn. To remain an insider, favored and undished,
posed a challenge, and it was this strange fidelity that
kept The Witch in friends. It was said that The Witch
had a secret boyfriend, a love whom we never saw. Questions about this unseen *amour* were rejoined with "I just
can't say," until we came to believe many things—that it
was a fabulous, perhaps famous, man, or that the lover
was somehow undesirable and thus too shameful to produce. These were mere suppositions, which neither Cap
nor Keith contradicted, though I suspected they knew
the truth. But I was yet a newcomer, and many histories
extended back beyond my appearance on the scene. I
was privy only to those tales in which I was a participant
or close observer; the rest was not my business. I learned
much later that these queens guarded their private
stories for two reasons—they were ashamed of the
shabby treatment they had given and received, and they
had to obscure, at all times, the lengths and depths to
which they had gone, lest their full histories should become known and rightly earn them the worst of epithets:
tired.

 At first I wondered at the secrecy and odd alliances,
wondered how Keith—who had seemed so plain when I
had first met him—had fallen into that particular, precious crowd, how he had become loyal to the physical
values so easily while it was obvious that he and the rest
of them were victims of those values as well. But Keith's

story was a story so common to us in the city that I was to hear it again and again. It was as if everyone had lived the same life: Keith had felt restless and lonely in that country college town, having met only men who, like myself, had merely filed his name in the bureau and forgotten it. So, one late spring day, following a midterm examination, Keith walked out of that brick and ivy lecture hall, looked around at the rich foliage and smiling students, and decided that enough was enough. San Francisco lay in waiting, the promise of steam, of love, of freedom. Within days he was there, excited and ready, and he plunged into a world of drugs, muscles, dancing, and sex. There was a time before I—or even Keith—arrived in the city when everything was new, and Keith molded his life to the priorities of that earlier era. Cap, who had been involved in that pioneering time, often told us that "the place was like a merry-go-round that got broken and couldn't stop." Keith's life had been like that, too—a circle of sex, disco, the gym, marches, petitions, drugs, tight jeans, and red plaid shirts. He began to fall in love and discovered it was never quite what he had expected. At that point the pain began, the common pain of wanting too much. He clung to his habits and friends, a comfortable niche from which any deviation was unnecessary. He worked harder, became more beautiful, took a nice apartment and furnished it well, had more sex, and waited in those long bathhouse halls for something new.

We spent long hours chatting about that wait, about our search for love. It was a collective endeavor, though so often it felt so frighteningly individual. Our lives revolved around the various methods of finding love and the many theories about how to keep it once found.

"Move in with him right away," said The Witch. "No, get to be friends, *then* lovers," Cap offered. Keith took a different tack: "Keep two or three boyfriends on the string at once and see who sticks it out." I listened closely and absorbed every opinion. My wait for love had begun those long years in the hills. Such a wait was destined to pay off handsomely. Something extraordinary would happen.

One day Cap asked us to ride with him to Twin Peaks after the gym. We all piled into his car and rolled up the steep roads that led to the summit. It was cold at the top. The wind lashed across the plateau as if furious over the obstruction of the hill. We stood beneath Sutro Tower and looked around us, in a 360-degree radius, unreal visions falling away from where we stood.

The tower had been built to serve San Francisco's television and radio stations but seemed more a giant work of New Wave art, like some lanky technological monster about to stomp down the hillside and send thousands of San Franciscans fleeing through the streets. I stood next to Cap and shivered. I worried that standing so close to all those radio and TV beams might cause cancer. Keith came up behind me and put his arms around me and declared, "It's too cold!"

It *was* cold, but I pulled myself free of his embrace and separated myself from the group. They chattered behind me like tourists, but I walked to the crest of the hill and choked back tears. That the sun was luminous on shimmering oceanic air was nothing to rejoice in; that

perfect cotton clouds lay against the horizon as if sten-
ciled by hand did not impress me. Such sights feed the
soul, but my soul had become as cold as that whipping
wind. I felt, for the moment, the way one feels when
something as necessary as a passport or driver's license is
gone—edgy with hopes that the item is simply misplaced,
not irretrievably lost. I stared at the jagged teeth of the
skyline and wondered who would ever put his arms
around me and warm my soul? If that happened, I knew
I could find my way. But for the afternoon, for the icy
minutes with my gym friends—who now accepted me as
one of their group—I would stand and stare at the city,
and at the water beyond, as lonely as I had ever been.

I broke my reverie when Cap shouted to me, "Come
here!" I shook myself free of melancholy and walked
back to the group, and suddenly I felt the heavy mood
begin to lighten, amazingly, unexpectedly.

Cap pointed to a great pillar of smoke rising somewhere near the wharf. It was as grey as fog. It rose
straight up until the top was caught on the wind through
the Golden Gate, after which it drifted east like summer
fog.

"It must be a tremendous fire," observed Keith.

"I wonder what's happened," said The Witch.

I shook my head and said nothing. I felt light-
headed, as if I were about to pull free of gravity and be
swept from the hill by that wind which scattered the
smoke and mussed Cap's golden hair. We stood at such a
dizzying height my head swam in the transparent atmosphere, buoyed by wind and friends and freedom. Here
I stood alone, waiting at a summit from which I saw the
ocean and towers of concrete, and I swelled in a sudden

sensation of harmony, as if pieces that had been stubbornly scattered were falling in place like magnets to steel.

I took a deep breath. I smiled. I foresaw the immediate future. Love was near, though I couldn't explain this sudden premonition.

The clear, cold late winter air, the smell of Cap's cigarette, the metallic tangle of the tower rising above us, the pale winter light, the rough hillside, the patches of dead weeds and grass, our red cheeks, the distant horizon—all of it created a sudden levity in which I felt utterly conscious and completely accessible. Naked and tender, life seemed wonderfully precarious, as if I might at any moment cast myself down the steep slope of the hill, gathering momentum like a snowball accruing energy until, in one vivid flash, I might vaporize and scatter across the city like mist on the wind.

This conscious emotion lasted several minutes. I examined my feelings, tried to find the reason for the sudden awareness, but there was no one thing, nothing specific to explain my mood. It was an accumulation of many things: the achievement of muscles; the acceptance of friends; the feeling of settlement and community; the burning awareness of the beauty around me.

The mood ended. Cap crushed out his cigarette, The Witch farted and laughed, and Keith grimaced in humored disgust. My feeling slipped away, bit by bit. By the time we climbed back into Cap's car and began to drive down into the city, the mood had completely vanished, but the memory of euphoria lingered like a woman's perfume in a room she vacated only minutes before.

For the next few weeks I led a plain life devoted to work and exercise. In evenings I read or watched televi-

•

sion. On weekends I attended movies with Keith and The
Witch, and on Sunday afternoons we strolled Castro
Street like a patrol, sitting on the bookstore steps or
pressing our bodies against the riotous crowd at Moby
Dick's.

Things were calm as winter passed into spring.
Nothing of moment happened, and the habits of work,
the gym, and a gentle social intercourse bred a feeling of
serenity. I wondered if I had found a balance.

6

It was late April when Stephen called me from Berkeley and asked me to come over that Saturday to see him. "You must come and have lunch," he insisted. "I'll pick you up at the BART station at twelve noon?"

I agreed and wondered why we had lost touch. My life had become so routine that I had let the rest of the world disappear. I had stopped remembering. When Saturday came it was warm and balmy: saltwater on the breeze. I opened my windows to let the air blow through. Somewhere wind chimes carried on the breeze in the minor mode, as melancholy a sound as high wind in the mountains. I stood at my window and looked out at the park, its greenery unchanged by spring, save for a fresh lime tint in the grass.

It all came back to me—Stephen's cheerfulness and vigor, and I was reminded of my longing and love for him, how I had sat alone for hours that one autumn and dreamed of something happening. But the mystique had gone. Now there were other matters at hand: how was Stephen looking these days? What sort of car was he driving? As I locked my apartment door and started down the stairs, I remembered those times spent running through the park on crisp autumn days or sitting up late talking. I stopped in the lobby of my building to wait for the mailman to finish stuffing the mailboxes, and I realized how very much my life had changed. No longer was I a college student waiting for life to begin. Now I dwelt within the daydream.

The mailman slammed the boxes, and I took my key and retrieved the mail: a letter from my grandmother, telling of the beds of iris, daffodil, and narcissus in bloom; a circular advertising a number of severe undergarments designed to reduce back strain or herniae; and an official-looking letter from my landlord informing me that the building had been sold and would be remodeled and that I was to vacate by June 1.

I got on the bus and transferred to the metro at Castro Station. Already the street was mobbed under the brilliant sunlight. The air was cool and damp, a relief under the hot sun. Flowers were everywhere—the corner vendors exploded with color: roses in red, yellow, pink, salmon, burgundy; carnations in white, pink, and green; tiger lilies, daisies, mums, tulips in lavender, cream, red, and flaming orange; purple strawflowers blended with tiny bouquets of violets; there were impatiens, freesias, and bundles of heather.

I left the metro at Powell Street and went downstairs to BART. The platforms were deserted, the trains empty. I boarded a short train and walked the length of three cars unable to select a seat just because there were so many. I finally sat and stared blankly at the dark tunnel as the train got underway. Across from me a lone fat black woman studied me for a moment, then turned back to the magazine she was reading. The train stopped once more and then sped into the tunnel beneath the bay. I took a deep breath and thought of the mud pressing on the outside of the tube buried beneath the water. I thought of an earthquake or a power failure. And then we emerged in Oakland, and I sat back and relaxed, counting the stops until Berkeley.

We rode above sections of Oakland that appeared like a war zone, so abandoned and decrepit were the buildings and streets. Here and there was a decent house or two, bustling with activity and surrounded by cars and children, looking like an outpost in a wilderness of burned-out storefronts, rotten wood-shingled homes, their front steps collapsed, their facades leaning dangerously into the streets. A column of smoke rose from a block in the distance, and I had a momentary glimpse of flashing red lights. Then the train plunged back into darkness below ground, and when I emerged from the Berkeley station, I found Stephen standing there smiling and waving, as handsome and cheerful as I remembered.

"Damn it's good to see you!" Stephen exclaimed as he put his arms around me and hugged me tight. "You're looking great."

"Thank you," I said. "You, too. You've put on weight."

He nodded. "Yeah, I stopped running so much. I just do a couple miles every other day or so now."

We walked down the street to his car. I smiled when I saw he was driving an Alfa Romeo Spyder. "This is really something," I said as we got in. The top was down, and we sped up the street, turned, then raced up into the

Berkeley hills. "First," he said, "we're going to the look-out, just like the first time you came to Berkeley." I smiled and nodded my head, then put my hand to my brow, trying to keep the wind from my eyes. We drove up into the hills, and Stephen handled the car with ease as we sped around sharp curves and steep, narrow lanes. The higher we climbed the grander the homes became, nestled among tall, draping eucalyptus and heavy, wide oaks. We alternated between the deep cool shadows of the trees and wide open spaces offering shocking views of the bay. Finally we left the luxurious cedar and glass mansions behind and headed toward the crest of the hills high above the university campus. And then he turned the car off the road and shut off the engine. It was cooler and breezier so high, and we climbed out of the car and made our way to the precipice where we had come so many months before.

I shook my head in awe at the spectacular vista that stretched below us. From Palo Alto to San Francisco to Mount Tamalpais, the view was unobstructed. The three bridges hung across a bay both emerald and azure, and the islands—Alcatraz, Yerba Buena, and Treasure—stood out in relief against the turquoise bay.

After a while we headed back down the hills, stopping at Stephen's house. We went inside and found Julie setting a table of smoked salmon, ham, English water crackers, cheeses, sliced apple, pâté, baguette, hot tea, and white wine. "Hello, and my god! What a feast," I said when I saw her. For some reason I hadn't realized that Stephen's wife would be there. I chastised myself for self-centeredness.

Stephen said, "Hi, honey," and kissed her on the cheek. I had never met Julie, had only heard tell of her that day Stephen had announced their engagement. It occurred to me how preoccupied with escaping that country town I had been that I'd had no interest in meeting Julie or in learning anything about her. The young woman who sat across from me was not more than a girl, really, but her eyes sparkled energy, and her lips parted in frequent smiles. Wrapped in a loose chignon, her black hair added an air of maturity to her girlish appearance. She was small—my parents would have used the word "petite" to describe her tiny lean frame, which was draped that Saturday afternoon in loose cotton pants and a raw silk half-dress worn as a shirt, tied at the waist with a red scarf. Despite an urge to be catty, I liked her.

"I just had an eviction notice this morning," I was telling Stephen as I studied Julie's clothes and poise. She filled our glasses with wine. "And so I'm going to have to find another apartment by the first of June."

"Will that be enough time?" asked Julie as she seated herself and sipped her wine.

I nodded and asked Stephen where his folks were; the house seemed deserted. "Gone to Europe for the summer," he said. "Mother has a cousin in Marseilles, so they left last week and won't be back until October. They plan to do both the Salzburg festival *and* Oktoberfest in Munich. It's been Mother's dream to spend a long time in Europe. Now that Julie and I are here to watch the house, it may be the trend for them to travel a lot. There's been talk of India and Nepal, one of those long exotic expeditions all their friends are doing now."

I nodded and tasted the pâté, spreading it on a chunk of torn baguette. "Well, I'm working downtown in customer service and going to the gym, and, well . . . you know."

"What about Ann?" Stephen asked. "Have you heard anything from her?"

I shook my head. "Not since I last saw her here. She helped me find my apartment, you know, and then she was going to move to Massachusetts and live with her aunt. Or was it her grandmother? I can't remember . . ."

"She hasn't written or called?" Stephen asked.

"No," I said. I suddenly felt as though I were under scrutiny. "I suppose I ought to write her myself . . . it hadn't really occurred to me."

Julie nodded. "Where are you going to look for a place to live?"

"Probably in the Castro," I said, and I noticed my own inflection, a stress on the final word, as if to impress upon her the blatant truth of my life in San Francisco.

"Isn't it getting awfully dangerous over there?" she asked.

I shook my head. "Not if you watch out."

Both she and Stephen nodded in unison. Did I see smugness in their faces? "Well, look," Julie said. "When you find your new place, let Stephen know, and we'll have a housewarming for you."

I smiled. "That's very thoughtful."

"Do you have a boyfriend?" Julie asked.

I shook my head and felt bad, for her tone betrayed assumption—presumption—as though it were a matter of course. So there it was again. "I'm looking," I said lightheartedly, and Julie smiled and nodded. I felt sad and irritated. And then I understood my half-felt resentment and my vague subtle discomfort. I *was* under scrutiny, though not on purpose. They couldn't help but condescend; theirs was the dominant way. I felt very angry then, but not with them in particular. I controlled my feelings and ate more smoked salmon. Julie refilled my wine glass, and the conversation turned to the weather, to the promise of summer. Stephen told Julie about our ride into the hills, and while they talked, I planned my escape. I wanted to retreat to the city as soon as I could. Their pleasantries and fine food and serene household set me on edge and filled me with a sense of imminent danger. As they talked, I drank more wine and noticed that they seemed much farther away than the mere reach across the table. Julie appeared to grow smaller. Stephen seemed far away. My head ached, my eyes blurred, and I lost my appetite. I could hear what they were saying, something about rare skin cancers and pneumonias. They were talking about the rumors, I knew, and my mind was withdrawing from this hearty little scene, this afternoon tea, this business of manners and concern that was rooted not in anything that reflected my world, but that was deeply entrenched in their outlook on life. It was cold and dark in the house at that moment, and I looked past Julie's dark hair, out the window, beyond the branches that waved in the breeze. . . .

And then I was back, thanking them for the beautiful lunch but explaining that I had to get back to San Francisco to meet a friend for a workout at the gym. Stephen gave me a ride to the BART station, and I promised to call and visit more often. He drove, and I breathed a deep sigh of relief and hurried into the station. An odor of fumes and plastic washed over me, and with a doleful wail the train whooshed past me and stopped. I boarded it and sat in the nearest seat. The train sped away, stopping two or three times until finally emerging above West Oakland, above the war zone, the sight of which filled me with excitement and a deep feeling of welcome reassurance. There was danger and abandonment and destruction. Below the elevated tracks stretched block after block of empty houses that suggested happier times when children played ball in the streets, when old black women tended to flowers and herb gardens, a time when on a Saturday afternoon the women would set out the fixings for Sunday dinner, do their hair up in readiness for church, and, at sunset, finally relax after a long week of chores to ease into the glories that would be Sunday morning in church. Abandoned cars rusted in charred lots beside crumbling brick shops. The pavement in the streets was lifted and broken. Here and there, in those outposts of houses still inhabited, laundry fluttered in the breeze from ropes strung between broken posts. Shattered glass lay beneath open, black windows. But the streets were nearly clean, unlittered—the neighborhood had been abandoned for so long that all the litter had blown away, the cold wind of the bay reaching every gutter, every street corner. I stared down at the beauty of that forsaken neighborhood. Its discarded homes and desolate streets inspired me to see with precise clarity just what it was I had escaped when I left home and then that country town: suffocation.

I ran to the gym from the station. I stripped and put on my gym shorts and exercised for hours. No one I knew was there at that hour, except for Laine, who, for the first time, crossed the floor to me and said, "Hi, you're Keith's friend, aren't you?" I said yes and reminded him that we had met months before. "Oh, I know," he said. "I'm just a little too shy for my own good."

I nodded and remembered what The Witch had said about shyness. "Well, I understand," I said. "I'm such a newcomer that it's still a problem sometimes."

He nodded, glanced past my shoulder, and continued to stand there. It was uneasy between us. I said, "Where do you suppose everyone is today?"

He shook his head. "I wouldn't know. But it's nice to have the gym so quiet and empty."

I agreed, feeling that there was still an inexplicable tension between us, but I didn't care too much, so I said, "Well, I suppose we better take advantage of it and get back to work."

"Sure," he said and then went back to his workout routine. I watched him walk across the gym and wondered why he should choose to speak to me after such a long time. And it occurred to me that there was no one else there we knew—not Keith, not Cap, not The Witch. So I had been right. I had imagined that something about the group was not right, but beyond that I could think of nothing. I didn't have any facts.

I walked home late that afternoon, in the long dusk of late spring, early summer. I imagined what lay ahead in just a few weeks—the long hours of summer evenings, the relaxed pace, the influx of tourists in the Castro, somnolent afternoons at the beach at Land's End, drowsing in the hypnotic wash of waves breaking on the rocks. And then, later on, the sudden interruption of fair days by the fog, which would roll in before dusk and envelop the city in a thick hush, until finally, some unspecified day in September, the fog would retreat for another year and make way for the city's true summer, the dank and titian richness of Indian summer. I remembered how different the seasons had been in the country, how Stephen and I had walked for hours in the autumnal heat, how I had sweated through summers silent and heavy.

I arrived at my apartment and looked around, with

eyes now aware of the move soon to come. I examined the plain walls and bare wood floors, the ratty couch and two overstuffed chairs, the wide bed heaped with soft down pillows and discarded clothes. It hadn't meant much. I had spent little time there except for those long winter weekends, and then I had mostly slept in a deep, depressed slumber. I was eager to find an apartment in the Castro, perhaps with a view.

I remembered Stephen's questions about Ann, so I went to the phone and dialed the Massachusetts number I found in my address book. After many rings she finally answered.

"Ann!" I exclaimed. "It's me! I thought you weren't going to answer."

"Hello! This place is so big it sometimes takes a while to reach a phone," she said. Her voice was rich and sounded happy.

"Must be a palace if it takes a dozen rings to run to the phone."

"We do *not* run in the house," she said in a mock patrician tone. "How the hell *are* you? You're still in San Francisco, right?"

"Yes, still here," I answered. "But I'm going to move to a new apartment soon, have to leave this place that you found for me, it's been sold."

"Too bad, it was cute. Did you ever do anything with it?"

I looked at the bare, dusty floors and noticed the pile of dishes in the sink. "Oh yes," I answered. "It's really a lovely place now, the right colors, nice rugs . . . you know the look."

"Hmm," she intoned. "Well, you'll do it again. What's up? Nothing's wrong, is there?"

"No, not at all. I visited Stephen and his *wife* in Berkeley today, and he asked about you, so it made me remember our good times together. I just called to say hello and to tell you I'll put a check in the mail for part of the loan you made me. I'm sorry to have taken so long . . . frankly I forgot."

"Oh fine," she said. "So you forget about me until Stephen asks after me and you discover that you don't know the least thing about how I've been and you develop a guilty conscience about the money?" She was only half-joking.

"Hold it," I said. "*My* phone rings, too. And I do receive mail here as well . . ."

"Okay! Truce! New topic. Don't pay me back, ever. I insist. My aunt has given me more money than I know what to do with. So that's that, and not another word. Use the money for your new place. Now, what are your plans? For the future? Job? Career? Any love life?"

I hesitated. "Well . . . I have an okay job downtown in this huge ugly company, which pays the bills, but my goal of course is wealth, by hook or by crook, so that I can get to that last question, find a lover. I spend a lot of time at the gym so I'll pass the fitness qualifications—"

"What?" she interrupted. "Qualifications?"

"For a lover," I said.

"Oh . . ." she said. "So you have to have too much money and too much body to get a lover. Is that how it works?"

"Well, don't take it so seriously," I said. "I was just talking . . ."

"Of course, just talk," she laughed. Then there was silence. Then she said, "Are you being careful?"

"Of course," I said, though I wasn't sure of her

meaning, but I didn't care to find out. There had been those rumors of disease. We began to reminisce about our lives in college, and after exhausting our memories, we hung up.

I sat for a few minutes and watched twilight settle through the windows. Keith phoned and suggested we meet for drinks at the Cafe San Marcos. I agreed and headed out the door. I'd had enough of memories and old friends for one day.

A relaxed, elegant crowd hummed in quiet conversation when I arrived at the bar. Keith was waiting for me, and we found chairs near a window overlooking the street. Throngs of men crossed Market Street and strolled out of view just as they entered Castro Street. The warm day had driven everyone outdoors, and some men still strolled shirtless, their chests like trophies on display. Glittering lights cascaded down Twin Peaks, crowned by that huge metallic transmitter blinking its red lights eerily into the spring night. Someone once said that Sutro Tower had originally been planned to resemble the Eiffel Tower, but instead it resembled a giant bobby pin. I thought of that day we had stood beneath that tower not long ago, when I had felt as though I might fly. My eyes lingered for a moment longer on the hills of Twin Peaks, and I remembered having read of an original plan to construct an outdoor amphitheater on its slopes.

Keith disturbed my phantom reverie by raising his wine glass and toasting, "Here's to Sunday!"

"Yes, Sunday, another day!" I agreed, already eager to assign this Saturday to the past. I looked around the bar, through the haze of cigarette smoke, and saw the crowds pouring in, appareled in the latest and finest fashions. That bar drew both an older and a younger crowd. One was stylish and rich, the other merely stylish. It always raised our spirits to pass a few hours in that place, to sigh and look and wonder what it would be like to have too much money.

And then two painfully thin pretty boys took seats behind us, exclaiming and declaiming in loud tones of voice about this or that sale downtown, about such and such a designer. Names fell from their lips like so much spit: Klein, Ruffini, Vidal, Stravinsky, Warhol, Leontyne, Hellman, Holleran, Trocadero, Onassis, Radziwill, Capote, Streisand, Summers, and Faithfull; St. Thomas, Haiti, Marbella, and Mykonos; Mother Lode, Gold's, Chez Panisse, Chasen's, and *Firenze.* I put my finger over my lips, and Keith grew silent. I turned my head just so, and listened: " . . . oh, gracious no! They've all had something like four hundred men a week! Truly! It's too much, that's all . . . of course not, darling! . . . well, isn't it just too perfect that a *gay* cancer should show up in *violet* spots?"

I spilled my wine as they erupted into fits of giggles, and Keith urged me to repeat it. "I didn't hear it!" he protested. "Tell me!" But I couldn't say a word. I was sick at my stomach again.

I suggested we move to another spot, and with a look of irritation and disgust, Keith got up and followed me across the bar. When I refused to explain myself, he let the matter drop, and then, as we stood in the corner and stared out at the room, we were joined by The Witch and a companion, a young man about twenty-three with striking auburn hair, gentle green eyes, and the fairest, most disarming smile in the room.

"This is Cole," The Witch said to me. I smiled and

shook his hand—firm, silky, electrified. The Witch turned to Keith and began talking about something I didn't care about. Instead I studied Cole, studied the way his lips moved up and down over his teeth as he smiled, the way his auburn moustache grew just below the corners of his mouth, the way his golden skin suggested freckles around the nose, though his complexion was without blemish. I stood and looked at him without speaking. He listened to The Witch and to Keith as they carried on. He paid no attention to my scrutiny, though I knew he was aware of it.

Two drinks later we were all talking at once. The gossip from the gym was hashed through. Everyone in the bar was dished and trashed and ready in our estimation to be hauled off to the guillotine. I began to feel strangely self-conscious about our cattiness and bitchiness. Cole did not participate in the snide remarks to any great degree. Mostly he laughed and glanced around the room. By the time the subject turned to the interior decor, I was in love. And the subject reminded me I needed an apartment.

"Oh, I have to find a new apartment!" I declared. The conversation halted, and for the first time Cole perked up.

"Where do you want to live?" he asked.

"Here in the Castro, if possible."

"And with a view, too," Keith added.

"I know a place," Cole said. "Up on Castro on the side of the hill—a fantastic view, too."

"For nine thousand dollars a week?" The Witch snarled.

"It's reasonable," Cole said. "A small one-bedroom with—"

Cole stopped midsentence and stared. His eyes were focused at the top of the stairs where they led up into the bar from the street. Keith stared there as well. I muttered, "What's wrong?," but Cole was hastily scribbling his phone number on a slip of paper. He handed it to me and said, "Call me about that apartment tomorrow." And he was hurrying across the room to the stairs. I observed this mysterious behavior with great curiosity. Both Keith and The Witch looked stricken with panic, and I suddenly recognized who it was that was turning his back to us as he followed Cole down the stairs. It was Laine.

"What was that about?" I asked, but The Witch had gathered his jacket and gone, leaving only Keith, who refused to explain. "I really don't know," he said.

"But why did you look so shocked yourself?" I asked.

"Because Cole acted so strange, so fast."

He was lying. I couldn't sit there a moment longer. Keith's silence bothered me—obviously another social secret. "Then I'm leaving," I announced, and I left.

I stepped into Market Street and wondered what to do next. I was too energetic to go home, yet the alternative of visiting the baths no longer appealed. That life seemed already a thing of the past, though it had been only weeks since I had indulged that ceaseless nightlife. But the rumors had increased; apprehension was taking hold. I could never have known, as I stood there on Market Street deciding which way to turn, how very soon I would enter a purgatory of neutrality, in which even the slightest caress aroused either the pain of loss or the fear of contagion.

But nonesuch troubles engaged me that night. I had only to decide my next move. Indecision won, and so I headed reluctantly toward my apartment. I walked along Castro Street toward Haight, and I felt a chill. I watched the streets carefully as I went. Every shadow concealed phantoms or violence. Every stirring of the breeze in the low branches of the trees signaled an alert: beware. I breathed deeply and tried to lift my heavy mood. I felt prescient, tired, and then calm, for I foresaw once again a future of immense and immediate discovery, and I suspected it had to do with Cole, whose face I envisioned and whose breath I imagined against my cheek.

A romantic mood overtook my dreams that night: I sat on my bed, and Cole came to me, but I sat still and said nothing. Cole whispered to me, but I heard nothing. I felt as if I were trapped in a tiny black box, one side of which opened into a steep funnel. I had only to curl myself into a ball and roll out of the box and down the sides of the funnel until I arrived in a land of grasses and rivers, tall trees and a town nearby—it was the countryside of that town I had escaped. I walked along its streets with Cole beside me, like Stephen. I felt expansion in my chest, a feeling of complete largesse. It seemed nothing could upset the serenity, the balance.

On Sunday morning I awoke slowly, taking my time to let the pertinent daytime facts filter in: sunshine; clear blue skies; warmth, even a warm breeze; the smell of fresh grass and the smell of coffee. I eventually opened my eyes and sat up in bed. I reached to the stack of books beside the bed and tried to decide what to read. There were too many books, all only half-finished—Stendahl, Balzac, *Dune*, Gluck. I gave up in desperation and turned the television on. Rex Humbard filled the room with words of heavenly hope, and I smiled and nodded my head; it was just what I wanted. I scratched my balls and went into the bathroom and took a long piss. A choir sang "Blessed Assurance," and then the Reverend Humbard said a benediction, *May the Lord look down upon us and bless us this morning that we might praise His name. Amen.* I felt uplifted as I turned the shower on and scrubbed my ass. I couldn't hear the TV anymore, so I sang at the top of my lungs: *Amazing grace how sweet the sound . . .* Then I burst into Cavaradossi's "Vittoria" from *Tosca: L'alba vindice appar che fa gli empi tremar! Liberta sorge, crollan tirannidi!* Then I lapsed into my finale as the tortured, broken Tosca herself: *Vissi d'arte, vissi d'amore, non feci mai male ad anima viva!* I dressed, made coffee, and walked across the street to fetch a Sunday paper. Then I got down to business, scanning the classifieds for apartments, noting three possibilities. But I wanted to call Cole first.

"Hello?" he answered. "Who is this?"

He sounded very sleepy. "You said to phone today about the apartment," I said.

"Oh, sure, sorry," he said. "I'm still a little groggy. I haven't really gotten up yet."

"You want me to call back later?"

"If it's okay," he said. And then added, "Please."

I smiled as I hung up, thrilled at the inane interchange. I poured another cup of coffee and read Herb Caen's column. I read Dear Abby, scanned my horoscope, and decided it would be a tremendous day.

I called Cole an hour later, and he said he'd arranged for us to see the apartment in half an hour. I met him on the high block of Castro Street, and as soon as I saw the apartment, I offered to write a check and sign the lease. It was settled that I would move in on the fifteenth of May. I strolled around the empty place and stood beside the long windows looking out over the Castro, and, in the distance, the skyline of San Francisco. The tip was all I could see of the Pyramid as it emerged from a clump of skyscrapers, but the green dome of City Hall and the white square chunk of St. Mary's Cathedral were easily visible in the rolling cityscape. Dominating the foreground was the Mint, like a set from *Ben Hur*, and closer at hand the pink and blue marquee of the Castro Theatre stood like a sentinel announcing the neighborhood to the world, and I envisioned how it would look after dark, a bright deco strip adorning the lower corner of my window. Cole loved the apartment, and I extracted a promise that he would visit often. To me, that promise carried extraordinary hope and possibility.

Again I studied him, tried to discern just what it was about him. But there was nothing. He just seemed to radiate. He grinned and looked directly into my eyes. I smiled and felt things I hadn't felt since Stephen—obsession and pursuit—moods that had hibernated these couple of years, as if in a cocoon, weaving, slumbering, waiting. There was a hint of Germanic or Norwegian blood in Cole, in the round nose, the full and expressive lips, a broadness in the face. He smiled, a Saxon smile. Where was the goodwill? What was its source? For a moment I felt cynical, but he put his hand on my shoulder and said, "I'm happy you'll like it here." We left the apartment and went down to the lobby. Somewhere in the building a tape deck was going, playing Michael Jackson, then Evelyn King. I looked at Cole as we emerged onto the street, both of us stopping face to face.

"Well, I have to be going now," he said.

"Can't you join me for coffee for a few minutes?" I asked.

He shook his head; he could not. I watched him walk down the street, and then I followed. The day was warmer than any other that year, and the street was filled with perfect men leaning their bare torsos against store-fronts or lounging at the tiny plaza outside the bank. I sat on the steps of the bookstore and watched the men stroll past. I imagined those steps were like the Champs Ely-sées—if one sat there long enough, eventually the whole world would pass by.

How many hours did we eventually spend on those steps? How many months did we sit, as languid as lovers after orgasm, doing nothing but staring out into Castro Street, accepting everything that crossed our vision as utterly believable, including the decrepit old man who scooped up his poodle's poop with his bare hands and deposited it in the garbage bin? We saw everything from those steps, from which we declined every suggestion and every invitation with a haughtiness deserving of Cleopatra on her barge. We saw the world of the Castro change before our eyes: One season we reclined and observed tap-dancing blonds, leathermen, and drag queens, hundreds, even thousands of bare chests sporting hair, tattoos, pierced nipples (left and right), handkerchiefs and bandanas the colors of the rainbow and then some. By the next season we saw fear and caution, green and orange hair, too many police, young men shuffling with canes, an unusual outside-world mix of women and children, and men not clad in tight jeans, and a group of nervous, confused Filipino women wearing masks of white hankies over their noses and mouths as they stood awaiting the 24 Divisadero.

But on that afternoon, in that lingering season before the great transition, I sat and took the sun and thought of nothing but my satisfaction at having found the apartment and at having stumbled across Cole. Already I had formed hopes: a boyfriend and lover.

I sat for too long, until my legs ached and the cool wind had begun to sweep down from Twin Peaks. Keith eventually found his way to the steps that afternoon. I told him about the apartment, about Cole.

He shook his head. "Be careful with that one," he said.

"Explain yourself," I said.

He shook his head again. "I really don't want to. I'd rather just give you a friendly warning to avoid getting too hung up on Cole."

"Why?" I asked. "I'm already hung up on him. I feel like I've been waiting for this all my life. He looks at me like it might happen, too. Why shouldn't I?"

"Because there are good reasons not to," he said.

"Name one."

"Okay," he said. "Like the fact that Cole and Laine have been lovers on and off for years. And every time somebody gets involved with either one of them, they get dumped and the two get back together again."

"Are they on or off now?" I asked.

Keith shook his head and shrugged his shoulders.

"So I can go out with him," I said. "There's no harm in that, there can't be."

"You're not understanding," Keith said, the slightest irritation in his voice. "The thing is . . . what happens is . . . the new person is always a catalyst that spurs them back together. It's doubly damning."

I was silent for a moment. I understood what he meant, but I didn't accept it. I would simply handle things differently than others had. Finally I said, "I can't believe you'd tell me something like that. I'd expect you to keep that kind of gossip to yourself and encourage me—"

Keith cut me off, "You're too much. You're making this into something it isn't. No, you're making this up! You've barely met the guy. I'm telling you what everyone already knows. Just don't waste your time."

"You're all the same," I said, sadly, defensively.

"*You* complain too much about everything," Keith said. "You think that everyone in the city is bad, that everything is necessarily tainted and evil and conspiratorial just because it's in the city and not in the country. You've got to wake up, dear. This is real life, not what you expected, but real."

"That's horseshit," I said, though I believed otherwise. Keith was right in some ways, but wasn't his very advice and gossip evidence of precisely what he claimed I believed?

I sat still and thought for a moment. I saw Cole, the evening before, and that afternoon, in the empty apartment. I remembered his sudden departure from the bar the night before, his hasty dash for the stairs, chased by Laine. Perhaps Keith was right about that, but he didn't credit love with the power I knew it held, the miracle I was sure it could produce.

Finally I asked, "Why did Laine turn around and run out last night? And Cole, why did he look so distraught?"

Keith shrugged. "It's what I'm telling you."

I said nothing, keeping a silence to review everything I knew of Laine, but I knew nothing.

"Why is Laine so cold at the gym?" I asked. "Who doesn't he like?"

Keith shook his head. "He's unpredictable. His alliances shift . . . it depends on Cole."

"But Cole doesn't go to our gym . . ." I was thinking out loud. The word "alliance" lingered in my mind for a long moment, because I knew that our group, and all the men of all the gyms and bars, were divided into alliances that shifted inexplicably. I had never understood the motives, the seeming deceit and social treachery. But Laine had no alliances to our group. He stood apart. So I wondered: Was it something about Cap? About The Witch? About Keith himself?

"Just forget about it," Keith said so abruptly and so harshly that he aroused my anger.

"Forget about it? That's like asking me to just give up my whole life and go back and forget the reason I came here in the first place. Is there anything wrong in my trying it for once? There's so much cynicism here . . ."

Keith held up his hand, tried to calm me, but I went on: "You say I'm 'too much' or that I 'complain too much' about life in the city, that I think it's evil. But the truth of it is that I don't understand what I see going on. I've been getting to know you, all of you, and I've been trying to fit in with your values for a while, too. But it's not enough—it really isn't—because the values and the behavior are fucked up. I used to wonder why everyone at the gym and in the bars and baths was so goddamn rude, with horrible manners. For a while I've assumed it was survival tactics, life in the city, but now I think it's fear. Everyone's afraid of being rejected—or worse yet, being accepted, being happy. I'm not going to be afraid. I swear it, Keith. I want to try it with Cole . . ."

Keith interrupted me, "But has he given you *any* indication that he's even interested?"

"Not in so many words," I said. "But that's not the point. The point is I'm trying very hard not to be afraid to love him, just to try, even if I make it up . . ."

I stopped talking for a moment and felt the cool breeze of early evening turn cold on my cheek, on the backs of my hands.

"Wait a minute," Keith said. "You don't just select someone and then decide that he's going to be your lover. It just doesn't work that way."

"Oh, so am I being an idealist?" I asked. "Am I asking for too much from San Francisco? Is it ludicrous to want Cole? Look at this street here, look at it! There's a message here, it's telling us something we're not even hearing, something to do with hope and the chance to love each other, to make dreams into realities. All I want is to stop all this nonsense, to put aside this bad attitude and all this selfishness and just love the street . . . the spirits speaking to us from the trees . . . just to make a dream come alive."

Keith looked at me and then down at the sidewalk and said, "You're in trouble."

7

Then came romance, the heart of the matter, the cause for remembrance. It came in late spring, fresh and sudden like unexpected rain. It rained a great deal that particular season, and memories of Cole come rippled, like water on glass, as if everything happened just outside my window, I on the inside looking out at Cole and myself—dodging sudden downpours, or bending to study iris blossoms, or turning our faces together on a street corner, our eyes focused only on ourselves.

It was a mild, wet spring filled with gusts of wind, afternoons at the marina, Sunday mornings at tables bearing rich coffee, croissants, prosciutto, and butter. Cool mornings yielded to middays as glaring as sunshine on brass, as if God had stretched over the city a shimmering canopy of pale blue silk, pinned above the green hills of Marin and fastened beyond the distant mirages of Berkeley and Oakland. It was peaceful and blue, washed clean by cool breezes so mild they were like feathers against the cheek. The serenity I had glimpsed that afternoon atop Twin Peaks now filled me like a drug, and I consumed the spring like a drunkard his wine, that spring of warm rain and soft air, espresso and vanilla, cinnamon tea, and white crocus. Flowers were everywhere—alerting my senses, informing my delirium—gloriously abundant, tumbling from corner stands, grasped in tight fists clutched to the body, arranged in vivid displays everywhere. Grocers, too, abounded in freshness—crisp green parsley, early peaches and tomatoes just delivered from the warming valley, folded artichokes up from the coastal fields of Castroville and Pescadero.

We played symphonies on the stereo, Mahler and Mozart and Saint-Saëns. We took long walks through sweet air, our feet aching under the strain of distance, for we were ambitious, crossing town, climbing hills, exploring deserted parks. We examined dozens of tiny, luxuriant gardens fenced in iron. We noticed stained glass everywhere, and potted plants, and redwood decks suspended from uppermost angles of fine homes, decks upon which sat men in kimonos, men together or singly, sipping coffee, reading the papers, scrutinizing the skyline. We waved to them and received their blessings. Of course we talked of Paris and Hawaii, of Raphael and Picasso, of life's rich sadness and anger and piss-elegance. Happy and eager, we agreed on everything: that churches were basically evil; that Descartes had been right; that Al Parker was the hottest of the gay porn stars.

He took me to the ocean (he always said "the sea") to

walk barefoot in the surf. We drove aimlessly through the city in his car, and we spent hours doing nothing but searching out new views and interesting cafes. When we went to bed, after hours of watching old movies as we laughed and kissed and chatted, our eyes only occasionally seeking out the TV screen at critical moments of *The Women*, or *Sunset Boulevard*, or *Dark Victory*, I lay beside him and told myself that this was the payoff, jackpot, the reason I had waited through Stephen, through those lonely days in Berkeley, through months of torture at the gym.

The long coldness of hope began to thaw, draining into the warm swamp of pure life as it unfolded in my soul, on his lips, under my caress. Surely I had come to the end of some journey, some critical intersection from which led, now behind me, the long road that started in childhood restlessness, that had pushed me through those strange and lonesome teenage years beside the river, that twisted through college and Stephen like the tangled paths beneath the thickets of the grove, now so distantly removed—vague memories that suited old dreams, nothing more.

Everything was exciting after that. The sensations—of novelty, of electricity, of surprisingly easy intimacy—were so foreign and so welcome that I felt at first as if I had moved to another town—someplace where cool breezes washed the air ceaselessly and kept the sky as polished as the hardwood floors and beveled windows in my aunt's distant country lodge—a town so crisp and so steeped in exotic history (earthquakes, fires, epidemics) that we felt, often, as if we might, after all, escape the painful troubles of the mundane world.

In the mirrors of the gym I saw reflections of men whose beauty no longer astounded me in my new adoration of Cole. Those reflections twisted and melded, alternately distorting beauty and then restoring it. Cole was not strikingly beautiful, no perfect resurrection of a Greek sculpture, no muscle-bound god freshly leapt from the pages of glossy magazines. What he was—I recognized as I lay beside him one night and watched him fall asleep—was a man whose attraction resided not in physical attributes but in the beauty of a soul that loved life, that smiled at sunsets, at waves, at shadows beneath trees. Physically he was well set to be sure, having those basic qualities we admire in a man—the broad shoulders, the lean, tapering torso, not overly muscular. His hips were square and lean, his skin covered in soft auburn fur that, when a hand was passed over, gave rise to goose pimples.

His face was pretty, though one would never have exclaimed *gorgeous!*, nor have counseled him to enter the world of modeling. His was the face of a boy who had become a man, alternately stern and playful, taking only a moment to shift from one mood to another, a nimbleness of expression that suggested moodiness. Yet here was an evenhanded man, one whose moods were never given to extremes, whose emotions did not play themselves out in peaks and valleys, climaxes and denouements. All of this was reflected in his physical carriage: slow decided movements, as if in no hurry whatsoever, under any circumstance. His plain attractiveness served, however, to inflame my feelings further, and I would, upon seeing him rise from a chair with dignified calm, hurl myself up like a panther sprung from a cage, or, upon witnessing his serene survey of a room or shop, I would rush in, babbling, carrying on in frenetic zeal.

His eyes were deep pools of mystery from which nothing was betrayed. One could stare into those green eyes—sometimes nearly turquoise—yet find no warmth, no emotion. Something was held in reserve there—a depth, a dark corner perhaps, to which the outside world had no access. It mattered little, this minor detail of something unknown, for his calm, impassioned nature set things right, always steadily on course. Our lovemaking was rich and varied, each of us willing to yield or to possess, talents that made each romantic encounter a great and sometimes bold adventure, for who would it be? Who would we be that night, ghosts or angels? Vampires or children?

After making love, he always leapt from bed to wash his face—the only sudden, habitual gesture he possessed. He would return moments later, his face pink from the revitalizing splash of cold water. He would lie down beside me again, hold me close, and whisper in my ear—sweet stories of childhood, of his growing up in Nevada, amidst pines and sudden thundershowers.

Days passed. They lengthened, the light falling gracefully later each day. The relationship blossomed, like a traveler's vacation planned over weary winter months, finally coming to fruition. After only four weeks our habits were established, as constant and reliable as the ordinary of the Mass, and we indulged our passions for rich food, flowers, and rooftop bars that afforded spectacular views of the city and bay. One evening we sat and stared out across the city, fifty floors below, and I turned to Cole and said, "Can I call you my boyfriend?"

He smiled and said, "If you like."

Though it was with less enthusiasm than I had hoped, his answer filled me with such exuberance I felt that were I to shatter the glass and leap into the raw air I might fly above the city like Peter Pan. My pleasure overwhelmed me for a moment, for a few minutes—for don't we all, at some point, recognize that we have always awaited the moment when we may attach such a name to a relationship, boyfriend, lover, husband, wife?—and I had to sit still, because being so very high in the skyscraper, vague movement could be felt as the building swayed in the winds, and I felt I might be sick. The feeling came and went.

"Can we go now?" he said then, and we gathered our jackets and left, descending so rapidly in the express elevator that I felt the nausea again. For a time after that evening, his enthusiasm equaled mine. Once I told him of my love for Yosemite, how I thought it was the prettiest spot on God's green earth. And for one weekend and two more evenings he bombarded me with questions about it, about its history, its scenery, was there a chance we might go on a short trip? When I had answered every question that fourth evening of his enthusiasm, he lowered his eyes and said for the first time, "I love you."

I trembled and wondered what to do. I did nothing but kiss him, and after that night, my ardor could not be diminished. I had the conviction of a martyr, so dedicated was I now to love. La Rochefoucauld has written: "Love may be delightful, but even more so are the ways in which it reveals itself."

It revealed itself so many times in those few, early weeks, the more so because my passion informed every action, every perception. Like a filter through which passes only the purest of a substance, I sifted through hours of conversations and glances to isolate each betrayal of love—the sigh, the faint glint in the eye, the sad gaze out the window at sunset.

I never thought our love was impossible in the manner of those men at the gym, who, through the burden of past experience, had come to rest on a plateau of high cynicism, from which issued their profoundly skeptical beliefs that love was an illusion, a false god, to be idolized perhaps—occasionally—as the mood of sexual arousal dictated. I ignored all such apprehensions, for what else could it be that buoyed me through the day as if I had lost thirty pounds?

The days were long and lingering, the light refusing to fade. After six weeks we were sleeping together frequently, Tuesdays being a fixed rendezvous, with Thursdays or Fridays as well, always Saturday night, rarely Sunday evening. On weekdays Cole arose early and hurried to his job. I didn't mind his early departures. I would roll over in bed to occupy the spot he had relinquished, still warm, the pillow still impressed with the shape of his head. Then, when I awoke later, I would lie in bed for a few minutes, examining every detail of the previous night, remembering every touch, every caress, every soft word. Finally I would rise, shower, and rush to the metro to catch a train downtown to my job, always late it seemed then, and as the train jerked and sped through the tunnels, I replayed our conversations: "It was crazy growing up in Nevada," he told me. "Near Reno, there's still a strange, raw feeling, like someday someone might strike gold or silver." I asked, "From gambling?" He answered, "No, not gambling, not that at all. It's more a feeling of calm hopefulness, legal whorehouses—you know, a feeling that anything goes and that *anything* can lead you *anywhere*, like me to San Francisco."

I had asked him if, like so many of us, he had dreamt as a boy of escaping to the city.

"Never *escaping*," he said. "Not even going to the city, really. But I did have funny daydreams, fantasies of exotic illnesses, you know, that I might want to have a rare tropical disease which would alter my appearance so that people would whisper, 'What do you suppose could be wrong?' But that daydream didn't carry with it any idea of actually *being* sick, just of the romance or the melodrama of it."

"I used to feign illness so I could stay home and watch TV," I offered. "There was nothing I'd rather do than see those old Lucy shows, followed by Andy Griffith and 'Green Acres.'"

"Oh, I used to love Marcus Welby," Cole went on. "Every week a new rare disease."

Our conversation led to a litany of our favorite, now forgotten television programs—"The Doris Day Show," "The Bold Ones," "Police Woman," "Dark Shadows," "Gidget," "The Mod Squad," and "Medical Center." We both confessed how we had waited for those scenes in "Medical Center" when Chad Everett would wear surgical greens so tight they appeared to be painted on his thick, manly body, sexy enough to arouse our teenage passions into youthful erections for which there seemed no relief. I wondered at the similarity of our tastes, but not on a personal level—not at *his* level or at *mine*—but at *ours*, as gay men, as homosexuals. It seemed to me that every campy episode, every film (*Ben Hur, Hercules, The Sound of Music*) for which we shared a nostalgic reverence revealed a sensibility that spanned time and locale. Had it all been planned somehow? Had higher powers conspired to convert millions of America's sons and daughters to a new way of seeing?

Life went on. There was still the gym. Daily I went, still working out with Cap and Keith and The Witch. I told everyone of the affair, my tongue fluttering like a pennant in the breeze. Of my friends at the gym, Keith was supportive—though I never forgot (nor heeded) his warning. He would ask, with enthusiasm, about Cole, about our relationship, and he had a hunger for details—the size of Cole's penis, the type of sex we had. Had it advanced to a stage where we said "I love you" frequently? Were we talking of living together?

"Living together!" I exclaimed one day as we traded off at the bench press. "Heavens no! It's barely begun. I don't think I could live with someone for a long time."

"Then just how serious is it?" Keith asked, his face bent over me as he stood above me.

"Well," I grunted and heaved the bar. "It's at the point where we're definitely boyfriends, and I'd say 'lovers' is a good word to describe it now."

"Lovers?" Keith said. He took his place on the bench then and, staring up at me now, asked, "Does Cole consider you his lover, too?"

"I don't know," I said. "I suppose so . . ."

Keith grunted and hoisted the weight over his chest, then lowered it, raised it, pumped. He racked the bar and sat up panting and sweating. "Surely you must know how he feels *exactly*," Keith said.

The stressed word worried me. There was more than friendly inquiry here.

"He tells me he loves me," I answered. "We sleep together all the time."

"All the time?" Keith said.

"What are you driving at?" I said.

Keith smiled and said, "Nothing, just trying to get your goat, that's all."

I nodded and left to shower.

At first, then, it seemed there had been enthusiasm. Cap, too, asked after us, but I detected the same form that Keith often used, more than questions, less than innuendo. Cap's questions were not unlike Keith's: Are you lovers now? Does Cole spend much time with you? At your new place? Maybe you should think about living together?

The Witch, the friendliest of all, provided the most support. "I hope you two are getting along really well," he'd say, in the form of a question nonetheless, which, owing to his friendliness evoked the most complete responses. I'd nod my head and tell him what we had done that weekend before, or the night before, in shameless, intimate detail. The Witch always smiled and nodded, even patted me on the back once.

But very soon I noticed a withdrawal of my gym friends. One day, while working out with Keith, I realized that Cap and The Witch had come onto the exercise floor without speaking to us. They kept their distance—easily accomplished owing to the crowd that night.

Within days I realized that they were avoiding me. Not wishing to be hasty, I finally crossed to Cap one evening and asked him if I were paranoid—were they angry about something?—but he only shrugged his shoulders. When Keith came in I asked him, but he shook his head and said I was imagining things.

I ignored my feelings as nothing more than a bad hunch. Of course my friends were jealous, envious of my relationship with Cole. Hadn't they, after all, been making nosy inquiries, as if awaiting a failure? Was it not the nature of gossipy queens to doom all good relationships? I decided to discuss Cole with them no longer. Instead, I concentrated on my affection for Cole, and as I exercised at the gym, as I sat at my desk downtown, as I strolled the streets in cool reflection, my mind was filled with constant images of love.

I would think of our time together, or of a specific moment, like that weekend when we had walked aimlessly amongst the olive-grey shadows of the park. We had walked breathing eucalyptus, whispering "see that," and stopping, finally, to kiss beneath a tangle of elms and vines. We had brought his cat, Jezebel, with us, and it darted between our feet and sharpened its claws on my jeans as we embraced. I remembered how, later that day, we had taken long naps and eaten smoked salmon on the deck.

It was as if everything had been staged.

8

That summer I felt completely alive for the first time in my life. And although Cole spent only one or two nights a week with me by then (for it slowed down in early summer, a response to busy lives, I presumed), I moved through the city as if suspended by invisible energy forces, which, as I closed the door of my new apartment behind me and strode down the street to walk those four blocks to Cole's apartment above Market and Castro, en route to our Tuesday or Thursday night rendezvous, carried me down that steep hill, past the rows of tiny, exquisite shops, past the ice cream parlor and the cookie stand, blindly through the crowds of handsome men I no longer noticed.

I saw everyone on the street as co-conspirators, their hurried paces betraying their own enthusiasm to reach their lovers. The record store, the theater, the pizza shop—these loomed always as indicators that I was nearly there, and as I climbed the stairs to Cole's apartment, I broke into leaps of two or three steps at a time: Life was worth living. Cole opened the door that night near midsummer when I rapped on the wood in syncopation, and I put my arms around him and kissed him. "Hi," I said. "Love you."

"I know," said Cole as he disentangled himself from my grasp. "Me, too."

We lay in bed for a long time that evening, warm summer sounds drifting through the open windows, the rush of Market Street traffic creating a dull monotonous music that lulled us nearly to sleep, and when the phone rang at dusk, I turned over and slipped into sleep. Cole took the call in the front room and returned to the bedroom to wake me.

"You're going to have to go," said Cole as he shook my shoulder and brushed his lips across my forehead.

"Why?"

"That was Laine. He's on his way over."

I frowned. "Okay," I said as I sat up and rubbed my eyes. I looked at Cole and was startled by his face, which wore an expression of anxiety. "What's wrong?" I asked as I slipped my jeans on, laced my shoes, and buttoned my shirt.

Cole shook his head. "Nothing. He's just upset about something and needs to talk. It'll be much easier if I'm alone."

I nodded my head in understanding and kissed him before leaving. But I didn't leave the neighborhood. Something kept me there and forced me to hang back in the crowds emerging from the metro. For fifteen minutes I clung to the walls of the corner bank, my eyes fixed on Cole's windows. Then the door opened and Cole emerged. He had dressed and was descending the steps with some urgency. He stepped into the street, looked about him as if in search of something, then hailed a taxi. I saw his face the moment before he climbed into the cab, that face I loved so dearly, so sweet and alluring, now twisted in a grimace of worry and panic.

My shame at having spied on him forced me home, where I poured wine and sat beside the window. I would draw no conclusions. I loved Cole. My fingers tapped uneven rythmns against the goblet. My feet tapped the hardwood. I kept the apartment in darkness and merely stared at the street, trying in all my goodwill to feign calm, to block my mind of Keith's original warning, to put down those images that flickered in the back of my mind like some horrible diagnosis the patient prefers not to comprehend. I thought of the few weeks we had spent already. I remembered everything, the way I had called twice a day for a date that first week, the way he had finally agreed and, by the next week, had fallen into a congenial affair that sent my spirit soaring. I recalled every day, every moment of our eight weeks together, how we had walked the neighborhood on balmy evenings, how we had returned always to his apartment, where, as twilight filtered through the glass and breezes whispered in the paper shades, we had made love and watched the city come alive in glittering abandon.

It seemed suddenly as though it were over. I had had no word of discouragement, but there had been that face, that grimace, and that lie. Laine had not been on his way. I did not know a Cole whose face twisted in panic. I didn't know a Cole who lied, who hurried me away before a friend was to arrive, though no friend appeared. My mind settled on that word: friend. *Friend*. I knew that Laine and Cole were not friends. They were ex-lovers.

A mood of great transition overcame me as I sat staring out the window, as if in a moment I had become someone else. It was like that point when late afternoon suddenly becomes dark: a sudden shift of light, like a trick, producing in the ensuing minutes the experience of evening. I held this feeling at arm's length, refusing to recognize the moment of conversion. I could make up my mind—one could, of course, bully emotion with intellect—but would it not be foolish to allow oneself to be swayed by passing depression?

I dismissed my forebodings and went to bed. For a few minutes before falling asleep, I sat up and looked at the twinkling lights of the city skyline. The view reassured me, the cityscape so pretty. It held meaning for me, the meaning of fulfilled promise, of daydreams yet to come. I lay back and struggled with the pillows for a moment before I was completely in the soft embrace of supporting down and linen.

The next morning I awoke slowly. My eyes were leaden, glued shut so that I had to press them gently. Had I been crying in my sleep? I wondered. But then I saw the brilliance of a midsummer Wednesday morning and was renewed once again with energy. I dressed hastily and hurried to the office downtown, but the day—though warm and clear like hot icing on sweet rolls—passed slowly, dragging as if to postpone some unforeseen inevitability.

At lunch I sat in Portsmouth Square. I watched an

old Chinese man toss crumbs to pigeons, which rose and settled in an accordion of grey flutters. Traffic snarled and horns blared. The sun beat down as hot as any sun I had known in the country. There was no breeze, no cool air. I sat and kept my mind blank. I felt like smoking a cigarette. I crossed my arms and observed the thronging Chinese shuffling back and forth beyond the screen of pigeons moving ever to the right in pursuit of the ancient Chinese man as he left the square. In the distance I spotted a man from the gym, walking fast, a briefcase in his hand, his sportcoat folded over his arm, his tie pulled into a loose knot, his shirt open at the neck. I meant to call out to him, but he was too far away, so I was silent, watching as he disappeared round a corner. I got up and returned to the office, where, as the hours dragged as if awaiting a loved one in surgery, I snapped at my co-workers, drank too much coffee, and became less efficient as the afternoon wore on.

Finally, at a quarter to five, I dashed from the building and rushed to Market Street, descending to the metro and shoving myself aboard a train packed with dreary men and women who sweated in their unseasonable flannels. The prayer of fog was on everyone's lips as the crowded train headed out, passing and stopping at Powell Street, Civic Center, Van Ness Avenue, Church Street. At Castro Street the doors slid open and the train emptied all its men, vacating seats and clearing the aisles. Women moved to seat themselves as the nearly deserted train moved on.

I emerged on Castro Street and immediately looked up towards Cole's apartment. I pushed my feelings down and hurried to the gym. I needed to face the solidity of iron and steel, for I could not face the vacuous sentiment that tried to impress itself on my soul, the sensation that something that had never been recognized had vanished. I felt the way one feels upon waking from a vivid dream, as if the past weeks had been somehow imagined, a fantasy.

The intense heat had caused the power company to brown out sections of the city. The gym lay in silent semidarkness. Late afternoon light streamed through the front windows, illuminating the interior, which became more shadowed as one moved through the exercises. The dead silence intensified any sound—heavy breathing, sudden grunts, gossipy banter, the dull chimes of metal striking metal. For the first time I heard the whir of the cables as I came to work out beside Cap and The Witch, who were already in the midst of a very hard session. I tried to converse with them, but their concentration was on the weights and nothing else, so I exercised alone.

I followed Cap and The Witch around the darkened gym, selecting exercise equipment adjacent to theirs, but conversation wasn't easy. When Laine entered the gym, his bag slung over his shoulder, his hair across his forehead, I watched as Cap leaned over and whispered into The Witch's ear. The Witch turned his head to the front of the gym, the movement of his head as it swiveled as slow and calculated as that of an actress on the stage about to deliver a stunning soliloquoy. Nothing was said, but eyes froze in mirrors—Cap's on The Witch, The Witch's on Laine, and Laine's on me.

I shrank from Laine's gaze, so piercing that I felt needles in my eyes. I blinked and looked away. I saw in another mirror that The Witch was now looking at me. I shifted my eyes to yet another mirror, so that I could see Laine undetected, but he had turned and left the gym.

I couldn't stand the confusion any longer, so I went directly over to Cap and asked, "Do you guys know what's going on?"

Cap shrugged his shoulders and looked at The Witch, who finished a heavy military press. I waited until he racked the weight and then asked him, "Do *you* know what's going on?"

The Witch looked stung. "Look," he said to me between deep breaths. "I don't know what you think you're doing, but it's not going to work with me, not all this naïveté. I know for a fact that Keith warned you about Cole, so if you don't know by now that Cole and Laine are lovers, then you're a stupid idiot."

I raised my eyebrows and cowered. Anger rose and fell away. "But that's over. Keith told me that, too. And Cole and I have been seeing each other for two months now. We're boyfriends. We say so!" I shrugged my shoulders.

But The Witch bristled and grew fangs. Cap stepped back and wrestled with the barbell in private isolation. The Witch's eyes became darker. "I like you," he said to me. "And because of that, I'm going to offer you some advice that you'd be well served to remember in life. Don't trust anyone. Confide in no one. Always remember intimacy is painful and wastes time. And never forget to fight, manipulate, and reward. If you'll live by those rules, you'll survive. If not, well, then . . ."

My face was twisted in a grimace of confusion as well as of great curiosity. I could see myself in the mirrors, my face an open question. What were these people doing?

Then The Witch said, "And that's all I have to say about it. I'm telling you point-blank, don't ever talk to me again."

I put my hands out, palms up. I shrugged my shoulders and said, "But . . ." But The Witch walked away. I looked at Cap and opened my mouth to ask him to please explain, but he just shook his head, passed his open hand through the air as if in benediction and followed The Witch to the other side of the gym. They descended to the lower level to work on their washboard stomachs, and I stood leaning on a bench and wondering. I was trembling, and the sensation of dreaming was strong. The other men in the gym were far away. Suddenly the electricity was restored. Fluorescent light snapped on, and the stereo came on full blast, the momentary power surge amplifying the music painfully until the attendant rushed to turn down the volume.

I couldn't finish my workout. I had to leave. I dressed and walked home. The warm summer dusk calmed me as I walked, and I felt less unreal, less like I was sleepwalking. When I got to my apartment, I phoned Cole.

"Hi!" he said upon hearing my voice. "I was just thinking about you, because I have to cancel our date for tonight and tomorrow night. Something's come up, and I have to straighten it out."

"Oh . . ." was all I said. "All right, of course. You do what you have to. I've got plenty of things I need to do around the house. Call me later."

"Okay, sure," said Cole as he abruptly hung up.

I phoned Keith but got his answering machine instead. I left no message and hung up. The apartment was in need of cleaning, so I got out the scrub brushes and cleaning solutions and mops and rags and went to work. I scrubbed and dusted and polished, all the while thinking about the scene from *Mommie Dearest: It's not you I'm angry with, it's the dirt.*

Every fifteen minutes I phoned Keith, but he wasn't home. Every thirty minutes I phoned Cole, not home.

I turned the TV on without the sound and glanced at it while I polished the hardwood floor. I put Lou Reed on the stereo, then Marianne Faithfull, then *Hello Dolly!* At ten-thirty I put everything away, turned everything off, took a Valium, and went to bed.

I shall never forget my dream that night, so horrible did I feel on waking. I lived on another planet that night, in another dimension, in a world where cataclysmic changes occurred with frequency, without warning—an utterly normal thing there. I lived in a huge stone mansion filled with androids and mutants, and while I toured the slaves' quarters with my concubine, one such cataclysm occurred in the rear chambers of the mansion, changing the residents into other people and shifting dimensions so that each person within the mansion had given birth to six others residing in concurrent invisibility in parallel planes. I awoke in a state of panic and lay in bed for a long time, unwilling to rise and abandon the images that haunted me and made my heart race. Finally I forced myself out of bed and saw that late summer had arrived: the city was blanketed in thick, dripping fog.

The day was long and grueling. My co-workers grew more stupid and obnoxious. I ate sweet rolls and drank black coffee all morning. At lunch I stepped into an adult arcade and dropped quarters into a peep show. Two men and one woman cavorted on the tiny screen. Atop a pink comforter they fucked her in several positions, for eight quarters, until both men finally masturbated themselves onto the woman's breasts while she heaved her bosom and rubbed their semen onto her nipples and down her belly.

I wasn't excited. I was tired, weary, and confused. I left the arcade and walked the perimeter of that tiny square, all red and green, then returned to my office.

All afternoon I phoned Cole's apartment but hung up every time his line was engaged by the answering machine. I wanted only to hear his voice, not contact him, not then. I could have phoned his office, but I had to wait. I tried to reach Keith at his job, but personal calls were not put through. I finished the day at four-thirty and raced to the metro. I bypassed the gym and went directly home. There was a message on my machine from Cole: "Please meet me at the deli at seven o'clock. See you then."

It was ten past five. I hurried to the gym on a cloud of elation. Cole cared after all. I had worried over nothing. At the gym I exercised hard. I was full of energy. Between sets I walked to the front windows and stared out at the gloomy fog rolling in and covering the city, silencing it, casting a grey pallor across buildings and streets. None of the popular crowd was at the gym, obviating the need for confrontation. I was vigilant for Cap or The Witch or Laine, but they didn't show up that night. I paid no mind. I concentrated on exercise. By six-forty-five I was done and happy.

I sauntered those two blocks from the gym to the deli. I stopped and examined window displays. I calculated purchases—some linen placemats perhaps, a set of earthenware crockery, a vase of cut crystal or black ceramic. I stopped for a moment in the bookstore and fingered the newest volumes by Edmund White and Rita Mae Brown. I leafed through a collection of old physique photographs, the poses so silly and yet so enticing, remnants of an era before the lurid had become vulgar. I stepped back onto Market Street and felt the wind, cold on my face. I blinked and put my head down, pulled my jacket tight around my neck. I felt mist on the wind; the fog was really coming in.

At Castro Street I turned and walked past the theater, its bright lights mixing so artfully with the grey mist of foggy dusk that one suspected an art deco conspiracy on the part of Mother Nature. *Such silliness!* I berated myself at that thought, *such romance!*

But then I was at the door of the deli, and there was Cole, seated at a corner table beside the window. He smiled and waved me over. I strode up grinning, and seated myself, fumbling in my excitement with my jacket.

"Hi, baby," I said. "I'm glad you called. How are you?"

"Fine, I'm fine, okay . . . of course I'm fine," he said.

Immediately I said, "I love you."

He smiled and nodded. "Me, too."

The waiter was upon us. I ordered a salad, and Cole ordered soup. We sat in silence for a long moment, and then Cole asked me how I was.

"Fine," I answered. "A little busy, crazy, but okay." I couldn't say anything else. I couldn't ask if something was wrong. Perhaps I had, as I suspected, made it all up, the tension, the paranoia. The waiter brought our food, and for several minutes we ate in silence, pretending to enjoy our food, pretending to notice interesting characters who passed by the window in the falling dusk. With the heavy fog, it was exceptionally dark out, as if Christ had just been crucified.

Halfway through his bowl of soup Cole put down his spoon, wiped his mouth on the napkin, and said:

"I have to call this off."

I put another forkful of lettuce in my mouth and wondered at the tartness of the dressing.

"I do love you," Cole was saying, "but I'm getting back together with Laine."

I put down my fork and sipped my water. I felt crazy, but I feigned serenity. "You love him a lot, don't you?" I said.

He frowned and answered, "Yes, I do. We've been in love for years."

"And now you don't love me anymore," I stated.

Cole shook his head. "That's not true. I love you a great deal, but I'm getting back together with Laine. I've made promises."

I blinked and swallowed. I took another drink of water, put another forkful of lettuce in my mouth. I chewed it slowly, examining Cole's expression of utter calm. "Well," I said finally, "if anything changes, we'll get together?"

He nodded. "Of course, you'd be the first."

"Of course," I said.

I couldn't stay. We made promises, to call, to get together for a movie soon, to be *good, good friends*. Had a major earthquake destroyed the city in that moment, I would have leapt with glee into the nearest gash in the earth. I hated everyone I saw on the street that night, their faces fixed in smug half-smiles as they rushed to the arms of their faithful lovers. *Such queens!* I said to myself. *Look at them! Physical beauty and nothing else. No wonder they're falling apart.* Cars raced up and down the street with such haste I wondered what could be so important. Five seconds, ten seconds—such were the increments these people tried to save. Race to the red light five seconds ahead of the pack! Congratulations! Fight for a taxi! Scream in queenly hilarity! Hurl your pickup down the street and shout: *Faggot! Queer! Cocksucker!*

I passed a darkened storefront and saw my reflection in the glass, the image of a muscular man who was too attractive, a man who was *hot*, his crotch bulging, my arms swollen with muscle, my chest. My own beauty was grotesque, as distorted and disfigured as if I'd had a terrible accident. I turned around, walked back, and bought cookies. When those were eaten, I crossed the street and had a chocolate sundae, then an ice cream cone. I stopped at the liquor store and had a candy bar. I trudged up the hill to my perfectly lovely apartment and phoned Keith.

"I warned you this would happen," Keith said as I recounted the meeting with Cole. "They do the same fucking thing every time. I wish you'd listened to me."

"I wasn't wrong," I said. Then I felt a heavy mood, panic under pain. "You know, Keith, the other day in the gym, Cap and The Witch were very rude to me. Is this what it was about? Did they know that Cole was going to get together with Laine?"

Keith stammered, "Well . . . I suppose so . . ."

I suspected something. "What is it, Keith? What's going on?"

"Nothing that matters now," said Keith, his voice betraying whatever confidence he held.

"*What* doesn't matter now?" I said. "You'll tell me . . ."

Keith stumbled, "Not on the phone . . ."

"What is it?"

"I'm sorry," he began. "I warned you not to chase after Cole, but there was more than just his old relationship with Laine."

"Go on."

"The reason why The Witch gave you that little lecture at the gym is because he and Cole have been having a secret thing for several months, which, because of you, has just ended."

"What do you mean?" I asked, stupidly.

"Don't be naïve," Keith said. "The Witch has been in love with Cole for a long time. Why else do you think Laine is so cool towards all of us at the gym? Why do you think he goes in the other direction when he sees us all out together?"

"That's absurd . . ." I said.

"No. It's more complicated, because Cap and The Witch were lovers, too, remember?" I mumbled and listened to Keith. I turned the lights on in the apartment, obliterating the view, but I could see my own reflection in the glass—phone in hand—against the black backdrop of the cityscape. Keith was saying, " . . . so that's why Laine's been unfriendly all along. It's Cole who's fucked up, who does the sleeping around. Laine just waits it out. The Witch was playing the role of the other woman."

I said only, "That's sick."

Keith was quiet. I sat on the edge of my bed and stared out the window, the phone in my lap. I could hear Keith breathing on the other end of the line, and it irritated me.

"Why didn't you tell me all this before now?"

"I tried to warn you. But you were lovesick, you wouldn't listen to me! And now, of course, it's too late, because—"

"If you'd told me all of this I would have . . . this was my first boyfriend . . ." My hands shook, and the world seemed very far off, as if behind a screen. I waited a moment, taking a deep breath. I felt feverish. And then I scorned Keith, "Why didn't you tell me? You city people are so horrible, just awful—"

"Wait," Keith interrupted me, "you don't understand—"

"The Castro just sucks," I went on. "It's full of assholes who couldn't tell the truth if they tried, even when someone's feelings are riding on it. Where do these queens get their fucked-up values?"

"Come on," Keith interrupted. "You're just hurting . . . and you don't understand the whole thing anyway, you just don't know what you're talking about."

I felt sorry for him trying to console me when it was clear that my daydream was polluted by their values. "No, it's okay, I'm still your friend," I said. "I'll tell you something, though . . . now I understand how all those queens become so vicious and bitchy."

Then I stopped talking. In utter exhaustion I gave it up. And then the way became clear to me. "Nothing is final," I said.

Keith groaned. "Be realistic."

"Of course," I said. "I think I'm going to go to bed now."

"You don't understand the half of it," Keith said. "You just don't understand how complicated it all is. It's more than love affairs and unfaithfulness, and it's a lot more than competition between you and The Witch. Now it's more a matter of life and death. Tensions are rising. People are starting to change."

"Such melodrama, Keith, really," I said. I knew what he was trying to do, trying to forestall the impact of my "breakup" with Cole by distracting me with those terrifying tales. "But I'll be fine," I said. "We'll be just fine. I intend to have what I came to the city to get. I deserve it. Don't you see that? Finally I really feel like I deserve it. I've waited too long already."

"Don't pursue this," Keith said. "Please. You're living in a dreamworld. You're not upset because of all these silly romantic entanglements. You're upset because you want your little daydream to be perfect. It happens to everybody sometime. As soon as you come out, you look around all wide-eyed and say to yourself, 'Oh, boy, this is it!' But it's not real. It doesn't work. What can I say to shake you out of it?"

"It's okay," I said.

We hung up, and I made myself a cup of strong coffee. I turned the TV on and watched a rerun of "Father Knows Best." Then, too tired to undress, I curled up beneath the comforter and went to sleep.

I woke in the night, unable to sleep, my body overly warm, my face covered with sweat. I slipped out of bed and opened the window, then crawled back to bed and lay half-asleep until dreams came.

The next morning was still foggy. I dressed and went downtown. I looked at the paper. I studied the other passengers on the metro. I sat at my desk and answered correspondence about this chargeback or that purchase order. But beneath it all was Cole. I went through my datebook and filled in every little thing we had done in the past weeks, every moment, every walk, every date.

By Sunday afternoon I sat on the bookstore steps and knew that it could be done. I could exercise the sheer power of love. I leaned back on the steps and watched the men walk by. Surely these men—with all their peevish misunderstandings about the true nature of love—could never prevail against a man like me. For as sure as I was that the fog would roll down from Twin Peaks by midafternoon, I knew that my love was strong enough to reclaim Cole.

9

Once the gates of love have been opened, they cannot be closed. Once love is learned, there's no stopping the flow. This is what we mean when we say, "You never get over your first love."

I discussed love with everyone I could engage in conversation—secretaries at the office, so opinionated beside the water-cooler; strangers at the gym, relaxing in the sauna; sales clerks at Macy's; the mailman; customers at the office. I fell into the habit of viewing myself from two perspectives—one as a single man, who, when he came home to an empty bed, the sheets so cool, the pillows so perfectly piled up, looked into the mirror and saw the other man, the romantic whose floodgates were open and gushing.

The streets were suddenly populated by dozens of men who resembled Cole, men, who, by turn of head or slant of shoulder, caught my eye, and I believed or hoped, if only for a millisecond, that it was he. Though his apartment was easily seen and his phone easily rung, he seemed as remote and unreachable as a mountain in the Himalayas or a village in Nepal, yet everywhere I went—walking down streets at dusk, riding the metro, standing in line at the market—I thought I saw him, only to discover, of course, after feeling my heart skip a beat and my lips twitch into the anticipation of a smile, my eyes ready to sparkle, my mind running a hundred opening lines, that the man with the worn leather jacket or the fellow with the nonchalant stroll was not Cole, but was instead a stranger with familiar movements, but a stranger nonetheless, as boring, as hopeless, and as incapable of engaging my attention as a sidewalk evangelist at Union Square.

Nothing interested me. Theaters were full of empty seats. Television was loud and insipid. Those friends at the gym remained aloof, cool in their avoidance of political shifts, alliances, and regroupings. Even Keith kept his distance, lest he suffer guilt by association. Work was dull and tedious, and I was suddenly surrounded by happy, well-adjusted heterosexuals, who, though peers, seemed somehow advanced far beyond me in marriages, families, mortgages, and vacations.

I was alone, with nothing on my mind but the bare facts of the short affair. I failed to understand how Laine could win. That mystery—of Cole's preference—ached like beauty. I composed letters to him, which I tore into shreds the next morning. I bought dozens of books about relationships. I read the Bible, and I turned, for a few days, to the Church, though I was not religious. I would pace the marble floors of St. Mary's Cathedral, where, as tears decorated my face and the late afternoon sun streamed through in conspiratorial grandeur, I would stand at the southeast windows and look across the roof-tops of the city. I knew that out there, somewhere, Cole was moving, talking, perhaps buying groceries or flowers.

I found other churches as well, which I esteemed for Old World charm and comfortable reassurance. I began to go to St. Peter and Paul Church on Washington Square, its shadowed interior illuminated by hundreds of candles, one of which was mine, lighted with whispers of hope and longing. I was not Catholic, nor did I want to be, but I found that the sentiments surrounding saint-hood, martyrdom, and passion filled me with a sense of serenity as I grasped for any satisfaction in the sudden glare of summer light, when at last I would emerge from my reveries and turn against the cold western wind rush-ing in to reclaim the city by dusk.

I walked for miles across the city until exhaustion numbed my feelings. Those late summer walks were hard and tedious against the strong wind, which carried the fog to shroud the city. It was on one such windswept walk that I came to stand one evening on the street cor-ner opposite Cole's building at Market and Castro. The width and angularity of that intersection (which I now found so many reasons to cross) allowed one to stand, un-detected, among the mobs waiting to change buses, and look up at the side of his building, pink and white, its fa-cade punctuated by swaying palms. I stood and stared up at his windows. Cold wind swept off Twin Peaks. A young woman caught her skirt and scarf in the same sudden instant a gust of icy wind brushed past. I watched her stumble against the wind towards the bus, its open door offering light and warmth, one hand clutched at her flowing skirt, the other grasping at her neck. I looked up at his building again. A light had gone on in the kitchen, but I couldn't detect any movement through the window. The young woman shrieked, and I looked back towards the bus. The door was shutting just as she cleared the armory of newspaper boxes. The bus pulled away, and she stumbled into the street after it, too late. Her face was covered now with hair, unrestrained as she held herself together, hair blown around her pretty eyes and her red lips. She raised both fists to pound on the back of the bus in one last gesture, letting go her skirt—which billowed up around her hips as if to mock her earlier restraint—and releasing her scarf, which fluttered away in the next gust, waving down the street until it became soaked in the gutter before the theater. I looked away from the glaring pink and orange lights of the marquee and focused on Cole's building again, hoping, as I stood there shivering in the blasts of frigid ocean air, that through the window I might catch even a glimpse of him—bending, perhaps, to retrieve something from a lower cupboard, or, maybe, stretching his arms before the view of the street that opened out to him from within his apartment, that street on which I stood, cold and huddled against the side of the Twin Peaks Tavern, whose patrons reveled on the other side of the glass just inches from me in utter ignorance of my mood, my hope, my longing. But there was nothing to see. The light had been put out.

Then began my campaign to win him back.

I sent cards, short notes about this or that book I had read, nothing of importance. I began phoning again, when I suspected he was not at home, in order that I might leave messages on his answering machine. And when, out of courtesy, he returned my calls, I often wouldn't answer. Instead I let them be recorded on my answering machine until I accumulated several minutes of messages from Cole, which, when I felt lonely, I would play back.

I lived on messages and hope. Things would work out. I would wait. Soon we would meet again, for he was returning my calls, and sometimes we would chat, about the weather or our gyms or work, and I knew that a rendezvous, something, would be the next step. He would feel no pressure from me, but the fact of my persistence and loving kindness would, of course, dissuade him of Laine's love.

One cold, foggy day in late summer I went to the beach at Land's End to walk. There was glaring sun and fog and saltwater mist. Waves pounded on the rocks and washed away along sand so rich and so smooth it looked like burnished gold. The ocean was emerald, the sky purple, broken by brooding lavender clouds, shifting fogs, and winds that whipped mist like sugar crystals tossed in the air. But it was warm where the sun broke through. In a corner of the cove two young men lay beside a small mountain of rocks, their arms entwined. One lone elderly man lay in the nude as though under the heat of July. A few couples strolled arm in arm along the edge of the surf, watching the waves break on the reef. And I strolled along that beach, too, my hands in my pockets, my jacket and scarf bundled tight against the cold wind. Tears streamed down my face, but I walked on, oblivious, wondering what might happen next. For a long time I sat on a huge rock and stared at the emerald waves rolling in, imagined just getting up and walking into them and letting the undertow drag me out to sea. But I stopped and listened to the waves and asked myself if the sea wanted me, were the waves singing to me? But no, they just washed onto the beach and drained away, no meaning there. The sea didn't want me. I stared at the white-caps and thought that what I most wanted in life was love, that was all. Not death, not money or muscles, not even acceptance. Just love. So I got up and walked away from the ocean and began the hike back up the side of the hill. The two young men were leaving as well, and they strolled ahead of me, hand in hand, their heads inclined towards each other.

When I got home from the beach, there was a message from Cole: "Just calling to say hi. Give me a call tonight or I'll try to call you. I'd like to get together and do something with you real soon. Bye."

I rejoiced. I had been right. Cole had called and asked for a date. Had the sky rained pearls and gold dust I would not have been more jubilant, for it was a moment of translation, from the imagined to the substantial. I was bewitched that night, by powers and alchemies that shaped themselves around me like swirling brume, inveigling, beguiling, luring me, like Lorelei the ship to the reef, convincing me to believe that magnificent lie: the hoax of hope.

I phoned Keith. "I know you won't believe this, but Cole and I are getting back together again," I told him.

"I don't believe it, and neither do you," he said.

I explained it to him.

"Well . . . if that's the case, then good luck," said Keith.

I phoned Cole and thanked him for calling.

"I've been tired of our machines talking to each other, and I decided it's time for us to get together and actually do something," he said.

"Agreed. What to do?"

"Dinner? Saturday evening? Then we'll just take it from there, maybe a movie?" Cole said.

I agreed and hung up.

10

On Saturday mornings in San Francisco one regards early morning weather as an omen. But that Saturday I disregarded the dankness, the thick grey late-summer air that held the city as tight as a girdle. I ignored it and thought of only one thing: the date with Cole.

Everything I did that day is poorly remembered, perhaps because it was so utterly grey, so plain. There was coffee and the paper, errands and the bank, the gym, a nap, and fine clothes for dinner. There was worry and excitement, speculation and hope, but all recollections of that day are shrouded in a mood of obsession, as if I had smoked great mountains of hashish and thus remembered but one thing—*wanting*.

At dinner I met Cole just inside the door of a tiny restaurant. We talked of ordinary things—movies, television, books, boys. My mind ran opening lines like a ticker tape: . . . *I need to let you know . . . we should be more than friends . . .*

Instead, I ate my salad and discussed May Sarton. After dinner I waited for the affirmative clue, the word or gesture that would say *yes*. It came. He suggested we go to Nob Hill and watch dirty movies, maybe see the live sex act. "Of course," I said, for there it was.

And so the obsession blossomed. It was an intangible presence, like those guardian spirits that are said to hover above one's shoulder to guide one through life. We walked up Market Street, and I dropped back two paces to observe him as he moved in front of me. We got into his car and drove downtown, along Market Street, its lamps casting amber strobes in long intervals across his thighs. We passed behind the Opera House. Men and women crossed before the car in a blur of black and white. We waited at the light as the last of them passed, and he reached over and touched my leg.

It was a night like any other, a typical night, quite usual. Waves were pounding on the beach, cars were crashing into each other, women were kissing their husbands, and we were snarled in traffic, moving and stopping. Downtown, people slept in doorways; in hospitals people died. Babies cried, trees swung on the wind, and everywhere in the city, from churches to bedrooms to bars, eyes widened in hope.

We got to the theater, went in, and sat very near the front. A movie was half-finished, an old bad piece of S&M porno, quite silly. I held my breath and waited. The movie went off, and the lights went dark. The stage curtain opened, and a young man in jeans and a pink tank top sat on a bar chair, his legs spread provocatively, his fingers on his chest. Leaning close to Cole I whispered, "He's hot," and Cole nodded and whispered, "Sexy." The young man began to rub himself all over, began to strip, seducing the audience into rapt adoration. I looked at Cole, my friend, not my lover. He was staring at the stage. My obsession grew. The hope was limitless in that moment as I sat transfixed by the sight of Cole's hand, so close to mine. I envisioned my hope like fog—coursing outside the theater and down side streets, pouring onto Market, climbing to the Castro, dripping over South of Market.

I looked away. A young man who once cut my hair was leaning against the far wall, staring at the young man on stage, now fully naked, his hand moving up and down to the approving moan of the audience. I looked all around me, then down. I thought of the street outside, imagined my obsession flowing over the city, filling dark alleys and broad avenues, swallowing all those men I had been with in the beginning, all those trails and missed opportunities, all those memories of long summer nights at the grove when every stranger was Stephen, was freedom from that slow river town, my obsession covering every glance and whisper and every passing hope, that spirit of utter devotion, that fulfillment of the daydream.

Cole didn't know the strength of my hope, not then, not in that dark, warm, theater. Something had to happen. Something had to be *said*.

Cole looked around the theater. All eyes were focused on stage, but hands were mostly still. Cole leaned his mouth to my ear and whispered, "Aren't you suppose to masturbate with it? Isn't that the point?"

I shrugged my shoulders. Cole was aroused, but I wasn't going to have him; he was going to have himself.

He opened his jeans and I sat there and watched. I thought: *Get up and walk away.* But there was still time.

Suddenly the young performer groaned and ejaculated. Under the stage lights the fluid seemed brilliant, like liquid pearls. I turned my eyes back to *my friend.* In that moment I considered a hundred acts. Should I reach over and touch him? Should I lean over and kiss him?

Then he was leaning forward, then back, buttoning his jeans, whispering in my ear, "We either have to leave or go in the back, I can't stand this." He stood up and nodded his head toward the maze that led to the private cubicles in the back of the theater. He moved past me, stepped over my legs and past my feet, and crowded his way out of the row and down the aisle and into the maze. I started to shake my head and couldn't stop. *Get out!* I told myself. *Take a cab!* But I couldn't leave, no matter what happened. The building could have caught fire and been consumed, yet I could not have left. There were things yet to be said.

The movie began again. I got up and pushed my way out of the row. Someone yelled at me because my body was in the line of projection and thus cast a shadow across the screen. For a moment I caught myself out of the corner of my eye, a towering shadow moving across a backdrop of buttocks reddened by spanking. I stumbled into the aisle and stubbed my toe, reeling in pain against the wall to regain my balance, leaning there against the wall, breathing and staring at the orange rectangle: the door to the maze.

I moved toward that light away from the dark wall, away from the heavy velvet curtain redolent of dust, cigarettes, and men, and then I crossed the threshold and was there, passing the toilets and finding myself looming closer and larger as I confronted a long mirror set at the end of the first hall. Stopping, I looked left and right. There he was, leaning against the door to one of the cubicles, waiting.

I was crazy. I worried about a heart attack. I walked down the hall towards him, not looking at him. I brushed past him and looked into those turquoise eyes: need, recognition, unwillingness. I looked down and moved to the end of a hall and passed into a room that was pitch black. A groan and a sigh moved behind me. I stepped back into the hall. He was gone. I went back into the theater, and there he was, leaning against the wall. I went to him and smiled, as if it were nothing extraordinary that I should be chasing the man I loved through a porn theater, the man who had left me because of his fidelity to his lover. I told myself: *Leave.* But he stepped away, back into the maze, and I followed. I watched him disappear into a room with a tall man in a leather jacket.

I walked through the theater and into the lobby. I went to the bathroom and waited. I paced and kept calm. I hurled myself back into the theater just as he came out, emerging from the orange rectangle, a silhouette of love moving from the light into the shadow of the theater. He came to me and put his hand on my shoulder.

He said, "Tension?"

I looked at him and said nothing.

"I guess I should explain," he said. "But why are you so upset?"

"Hurt."

"Why?"

"Because it's a stranger!"

"Exactly," he said.

"Your faithfulness to Laine?"

"Let's go," he said. We walked out of the theater and began to walk up Powell Street against the wind. Near the car we stopped and faced each other.

"Don't you understand?" he asked. "It's just horniness, no meaning. With you it would have meaning. I couldn't do that to Laine."

I was silent. I could say nothing. It was *my* love, *my* obsession. Finally I said, "I thought we were going to try again."

He frowned and said, "Get in the car." We drove down Pine Street, past St. Francis Hospital. He made a gesture with his hand, hopeless, frustrated. "It's good, but . . ." He started shaking his head and couldn't stop.

I thought, *I love you.*

"Why can't we just be loving friends?" he asked. And then he added, "Who knows what will happen?"

I betrayed no emotion. We got out of the car at his place and walked to the corner store. He bought cigarette papers. He told me he was going to get high when he got home; he had to go out with Laine to the Eagle at midnight. He stopped me before I turned to walk away and kissed me lightly on the lips.

"I'm okay," I said. "Really."

"If you're not," he said, "call me, okay?"

"Okay." I walked away into the icy wind sweeping down from Twin Peaks. Beautiful young men walked past me, and I realized where I was once again, at the corner of Castro and Market. I walked towards the gym, for no reason, and tears streamed down my face. A pretty young man walked past and looked at me as though I were hideously disfigured: he could not bear my emotion. I turned and walked up Castro Street and pounded up the stairs and into my apartment, my new apartment, the place Cole had helped me find. It was as if I were surrounded by gossamer, so distant was the world, so dim the lights. I tried to focus on little things— the pattern in the floorboards, the drop of water on the bathroom mirror, the hole in the bath towel. I felt as if my memory had been washed away. I could not remember what I had done, where I had been. I turned on the phone machine and listened to Cole's message over and over: *Just calling to say hi. Give me a call tonight or I'll try to call you. I'd like to get together and do something with you real soon. Bye.* I reversed the tape again: *Just calling to say hi . . .*

I sat on the bed. I turned on the television and turned it off again. I tried not to cry. I dialed Ann's number in Massachusetts but hung up before it rang. I dialed Stephen's number. No answer. I started to dial Keith, then hung up. I dialed Cole's number. He knew who it was.

"I just called to say that everything's okay, really," I said weakly.

"What?"

"Everything's okay, I just wanted you to know. Is everything okay with you?"

"If it is with you," he said.

"When will we talk again?" I asked.

"Soon."

"Okay, fine."

"It's okay," he said. "I'll call you soon, I will."

He hung up. I sat still for a moment. Something crossed my mind, as midnight approached—to go south of Market, to intercept Cole and Laine. And then I was out the door. I hailed a taxi and told him to drive me south of Market. I felt tension as we entered that neighborhood—nerves, sexuality, leather, steam. At the stoplight at Folsom Street I leaned back and took a deep breath.

The light changed, and I told the cabdriver to hurry. He accelerated into the intersection and hurled the car round the corner. I slouched in the back seat. My stomach was a knot. I tried to focus my eyes and I told the driver to pull to the curb. I opened the door and vomited in the gutter. The cabbie tossed me some tissues and sped away, leaving me crouched on the curb.

I reeled into that night world between Howard and Harrison streets. I nearly lost my way in the darkness of an alley that was closed at one end, along which I saw glistening black leather and the glowing red tips of cigarettes. Passing bins of garbage which reeked and men who faced brick walls, I lurched along, emerging, finally, into Folsom Street. I walked into the Brig and began to drink. A dozen times in my mind I rehearsed a scene in which I encountered *my friend* Cole and his lover Laine and regarded them both with complete ease, proving that yes, I would be a *friend*. But they were not at the Brig. I studied every face, every gesture, every curl of cigarette smoke and every raucous laugh. I wanted to find them, but they weren't there. He had said they were going to the Eagle, not the Brig. But I didn't go there. I couldn't face them with vomit on my shirt, my eyes red with liquor. Instead I drank and drank, beer and more beer.

Eventually I took a cab and reeled into my apartment again. I stared out at the glittering lights of San Francisco and remembered how enchanting the skyline had once been to me. I shook myself and tried to remember the exact phrases Cole and I had exchanged that evening, the precise words. I turned the answering machine on, reversed the tape, and listened to his voice over and over again, ten, twelve times. I thought of the ocean, of the dark green waves, of mermaids singing into the night. I stepped into the closet and touched my leathers—chaps, cap, boots, jacket—and considered taking myself in leather-clad majesty and reigning into the Eagle—tough.

But I couldn't do it. I tried to cry again, but my eyes were dry. Something was finished, completely done—something more than a broken relationship. I felt in that moment that the ache of longing cut as deep as the spirit. This was no mere matter of the flesh, or even of emotion. Muscles, beauty, evanescent love, and passion would never fill the night. I was overwhelmed by a fury that—in an empty bedroom in the middle of a Saturday night—dissolved in an understanding that this life was as bankrupt as any of the lives I had left behind. I felt, as I looked beyond the twinkling lights of the city and above the thickening fog, that something absolutely new and utterly extraordinary would have to happen next.

The night sky was black velvet, the few stars diamond dust. I stared and felt my spirit unwinding from the tight, cold coil it had been—expanding, reaching across the city, through the fog, above the petty concerns in which I had immersed myself. And, quite suddenly, I understood that the purpose of life was not longing, but transcendence—communion with the stars that shimmered always, regardless of fog or storm, in that open galaxy beyond.